US, IN PROGRESS

Short Stories About Young Latinos

US,
IN PROGRESS

Short Stories About Young Latinos

LULU DELACRE

HARPER

An Imprint of HarperCollinsPublishers

Photo that inspired the portrait of Emilio
by Gladskikh Tatiana/Shutterstock.com
Photo that inspired the portrait of Marla
by Rachel Matos of theArtMuse.me
Photo that inspired the portrait of Güera
by Rachel Atkinson
Photos that inspired the portraits of Alina and Romina
by Flying Squid Studio
Photo that inspired the portrait of Luci
by Joaquín Medina and Kali Blocker
Photo that inspired the portrait of Pablito
by Thomas Schulz
Photo that inspired the portrait of Frank
by Vincent Hygonnet

Library of Congress Control Number: 2016949990
ISBN 978-0-06-239214-5 (hardback) — ISBN 978-0-06-239215-2 (pbk.)

Typography by Erin Fitzsimmons
21 22 23 24 PC/LSCH 10 9 8 7 6

First Edition

To the real twins behind "The Attack"
and to their mother, *con gran cariño —L.D.*

CONTENTS

INTRODUCTION

The first chapter in this book is also the story that inspired me to create this collection. "The Attack" tells the story of an encounter with the police gone wrong. It is a true story, and one that a family friend shared with me from her life. At the time I encouraged Guadalupe (not her real name) to go to the press, but she refused, not wanting to have additional complications with the police. Her choice to flee the United States and spare her sons further repercussions, rather than tell her story, left me unsettled. I firmly believed this story needed to be told. I started to read as much as I could about Latinos in the news. And a picture began to emerge that reinforced my belief that while we Latinos are an integral part of the American fabric and provide texture and richness to it, we remain elusive in children's books. So I set out to create a collection of stories that portray coming-of-age experiences in the context of current events that affect young Latinos in the United States. The collection shows geographic and cultural diversity. Stories of middle-class Tejanos are featured alongside those of first-generation, working-class Mexicans and Puerto Rican diaspora kids in Florida. In presenting a broad swath of Latinidad, I aim to show that we are not a monolithic group. All stories are based on either news articles or the personal experiences of my friends and acquaintances.

As I developed the collection, I chose to pair each story with a *refrán*. *Refranes* are Spanish sayings widely used throughout Latin America and often sprinkled in conversation. It takes less time to use a *refrán* to make a point than to find the right words to explain a complex situation. I'd like you, the reader, to think about the point each *refrán* makes in relationship to the story.

Finally, I decided to create mixed-media portraits of the main characters in the collection. The portraits give faces to the many young Latinos who are often invisible to mainstream America and who experience challenges similar to those described in the stories. I drew faces that show an array of feelings common to any young person, establishing a connection with the reader on an emotional level, and pulling him or her deeper into the stories.

Each portrait is made with three layers. Just as I began my research process with a true story or piece of reporting, so I began my illustrations: the base layer is torn newspaper, linking in this way expository and creative writing. The next layer is a pencil drawing on a translucent plastic sheet called *acetate*: the unfinished portrait of a main character. I purposely left the drawings undone to suggest that each young person is a work in progress. The last, and top, layer is rice paper pierced with tiny holes at equal intervals suggesting a graph. In places, the holes increase in number, subtly marking the growing presence of Latinos in the United States. This imagery shows that this population is not only tightly woven into the fabric of the United States, but that it adds complexity and beauty to our country.

I hope that after reading the collection and looking at the art, you will have a more nuanced view of the young Latinos growing up among us, and I hope that some stories will provide you with answers and others will pose questions.

Enjoy the stories! *¡Disfruta los cuentos!*

Lulu Delacre

THE ATTACK

De noche todos los gatos son pardos.

Emilio watched the steam rise from the hot iron as Mamá pressed the collar of Mr. Rodok's perfectly white shirt. She stared out the window of the laundry room at her old green van parked by the edge of the manicured lawn.

"As soon as we're done here, I'll drop you two home and head to the pharmacy," she told Emilio and José. "I need to get Tony's epilepsy medicine." Mamá frowned, and Emilio knew she worried about the medicine.

"Can we go with you?" asked José, standing by the tall double dryer. "To buy new school supplies?"

"Don't think so, *m'hijo*," Mamá said, wiping sweat beads from her forehead with the back of her hand. "Tell you what: On Saturday I'll take you and Emilio to the Minneapolis back-to-school fair for some free supplies. *¿Sí?*"

Emilio heard the eagerness in Mamá's voice, like she was offering a chocolate-covered almond instead of a stale peanut. He lifted his eyes from his book and saw his twin slide down against the dryer's door to land on the floor, sulking.

"Yeah, we'll find something," Emilio said to soothe José. Emilio knew how hard Mamá worked as a maid in ten different houses to make ends meet. Three of their older brothers were on their own. But since Papá had trouble holding down a job and Tony's was part-time because of his disability, Mamá was the main provider for the family. She went on vacation only every two years. That's when the bunch of them would pack into their van and drive the long way south to their parents' native Guanajuato in Mexico, to visit family and friends. Mamá said she didn't want her US-born sons to lose track of their roots.

"When school starts," José said as he jumped to his feet, "me and my friends Marco and Pablo are starting a *fútbol* club! Emilio will be in it too. Right, Emilio? Last year the teacher told us that you can be anything you want in America. And I'm going to be *una estrella del fútbol*."

"*¡Qué bueno!*" said Mamá. "Now come, my soccer star, and help me carry up these ironed clothes."

Today Mamá had insisted on bringing Emilio and José to work. Emilio had a cold, and even though they were already eleven, Mamá did not like to leave them alone in the house. Emilio knew why. He had once overheard Mamá talking to the neighbor about how special he and his brother were. *They are my* milagros, Mamá had said. The way Mamá told it, she'd known she would be having identical twins long before she had gone to the doctor. La Virgen de Guadalupe had told her so in a dream. She was old, fifty-one, and was not supposed to be able to have more children. After raising three boys and having to manage Tony's condition, she was also exhausted. Mamá said that when her *milagros* arrived, the light of day came into her life again.

Emilio smiled at the thought of being a miracle.

The twins ran upstairs as soon as they got home. Emilio went into their room first, wanting to see Tony before he left for work. Lately, he had noticed that Tony's seizures had become more frequent. His older brother would complain about how scary it was when the attacks came without warning. Tony said it was better to feel the trembling and chills in his body, the metallic taste in his mouth, than to be taken by surprise. The nasty symptoms allowed him to get ready. "It's horrible." Tony had tried to describe to Emilio what an epileptic attack was like. "It's like having a huge electric storm inside my head. An unstoppable storm."

Tony was coming out of the shower and reached for his meds on top of the chest of drawers. He found the vial empty.

"Mamá is bringing your prescription soon," Emilio said.

"That's right," agreed José, pulling Emilio by the shirt to coax him into playing an action video game next to him.

Tony finished getting dressed and headed downstairs for a snack before catching the bus. "Do you two want some pineapple?" he called from the kitchen. "I'm cutting up a new one that Mamá brought last night."

"No, thanks!" Emilio and José yelled at the same time. "*¡Gracias!*"

Emilio got up and went into the bathroom. On top of the toilet tank was Tony's MedicAlert bracelet. It was engraved with his condition, and he was supposed to wear it at all times. But his brother didn't like to shower with it. Emilio could hear his mother's voice in his head, upset with Tony for forgetting the bracelet in the bathroom.

"Tony!" Emilio hollered. "Your bracelet!"

Before Tony could answer, a loud thump came from downstairs, followed by a string of shattering noises. Emilio raced down the stairs and slid to a stop outside the small, dark kitchen. Tony was sprawled on the floor, clenching a bloody knife in his right fist—his eyelids fluttering, eyeballs rolling back. Pieces of pineapple were scattered across the kitchen. Emilio opened his mouth, wanting to call José, but nothing would come out. So he stood there, frozen. Suddenly he felt his twin's presence. He turned to see José springing from the stairs and lunging toward Tony, ready to take the knife out of his hand.

"No!" Emilio yelled. "Don't touch him! He could hurt you if he starts jerking around. I'll call nine-one-one!"

Within minutes, blaring sirens filled the air. Two officers from the station around the corner burst through the front door.

"Get out of the way!" said one of them, pushing Emilio to the side as soon as he saw Tony lying on the floor with the knife in his hand. The officers rushed into the kitchen to control the situation. They screamed at Tony and kicked him several times to make him release his tight grip on the knife. But instead the blows seemed to trigger another seizure. Tony flailed his arm and the knife's blade sliced into the leg of one of the officers.

"What an idiot!" the injured policeman cried, cursing under his breath.

Backup officers pushed their way into the house, yelling back and forth, one louder than the other. Emilio retreated to the foot of the stairs and crouched by the doorway, covering his ears, his eyes glued to the scene. José shouted through the commotion as he tried to explain his brother's condition to the police. And adding to the mayhem, a tall officer stormed into the house. She drew her gun and aimed it at Tony, who was now lying motionless and barely conscious on the linoleum floor.

"Don't shoot!" someone ordered. "Handcuff the guy and take him in. Charge him with assault on a law enforcement officer."

On that command, a policeman put Tony's arms behind his back, handcuffed him, and started to read him his rights.

"No!" screamed José. "He didn't mean it."

"He's sick," Emilio whispered. "He—he—has epilepsy."

Mamá pulled into the driveway to find Tony being pushed by his head into the backseat of a police car, its engine rumbling.

"*¡Ay, Diosito mío!*" Emilio heard her scream as she jumped out of her van, dropping Tony's medicine. "My God, what is going on?" She ran after the car as it rounded the corner. "Come back!" she cried again and again.

✳ ✳ ✳

From that day on, Emilio began to have nightmares. As days turned into weeks, the nightmares became more frequent and scarier. In the still of the night, he would wake up sobbing. When this happened, José would move to his side and lie quietly next to him until Emilio fell asleep again.

One night, Emilio could not go back to sleep. Even with José by his side he couldn't stop thinking about all the things that had happened since that awful afternoon. Their parents had received a letter from the police suing Tony for attempting to harm an officer. Their mother had held endless conversations with Tony's social worker, neurologist, and lawyer. The court date for Tony to defend himself was fast approaching. But even with the likely prospect of all charges being dropped and the lawsuit being dismissed because of Tony's medical condition, Papá had been threatening to leave the United States for good. He thought the police had singled them out and didn't feel welcome anymore.

Part of Emilio wanted to leave too. Go far, far away, to Mexico, where he wouldn't have to walk by the police station on his way home from school. Every time he did, his breathing became shallow, his skin felt clammy, and the blood drained from his face. But part of Emilio wanted to stay; he was sad for José, knowing how hard it would be for him to leave. Just two months into middle school, José was having a great time. He had joined a soccer club, just like he had dreamed about. He liked his teachers and had made many new friends. Not Emilio. At school, Emilio could hardly concentrate. He couldn't help but wonder why all of this had had to happen. If he hadn't called 911, Tony would have never been arrested. He replayed the scene in his head over and over, each time coming up with a different ending, one that did not involve Tony getting sent to jail, creating more problems for Mamá to try to solve. At times Emilio wondered: If he hadn't called, would José have been able to pry the knife out of Tony's hand safely? *Calling for help was the right thing to do!* José kept telling him. True, they had learned at school that in an emergency you called 911. But was that wrong? And what if Tony had been wearing his bracelet? Maybe then the officers would have understood right away that he was ill. In the end, Emilio knew, *he* was the one who'd chosen to make the call that had triggered the horrible events. No one else.

They are my milagros, Mamá always said. Some miracle he was.

Since school started, Emilio had been to the counselor's office many times. The counselor had asked endless questions, trying to figure out what was going on in his head. Why had his grades worsened? Why wasn't he engaged in school? Emilio was polite but refused to talk. He couldn't bear to say a single word that would remind him of the events of that afternoon. Each time someone brought up the subject, Emilio clammed up, stone-faced.

Outside, the sun rose. And at the first morning light Emilio felt a headache coming on.

José jumped out of bed. "Let's go, Emilio!" he exclaimed. "I have soccer practice at school today!"

Emilio got ready for school in wordless, mechanical motions. Later in the afternoon Mamá and Papá were meeting with his school counselor. What would come of it? Emilio wondered.

That evening, Emilio was home, helping to clear the dinner dishes along with José. It was then that Mamá gathered the family together. *"Vamos a rezar,"* Mamá said. "Let's pray." Emilio knew something was troubling Mamá. When she was troubled, she would urge the family to pray the rosary in the middle of the week. Emilio, José, Mamá, Papá, and Tony alternated Hail Marys for every single bead.

After they were done, Mamá leaned back in her chair.

"Listen, *niños,*" she said, measuring her words.

"Your father and I think you need to finish school in Mexico. Tony will stay here in the house with one of your older brothers. He needs the care that the county provides."

Emilio looked up, holding his breath.

"What?" José blurted from the edge of his seat. "You mean forever?"

"No, not forever. We'll drive back to visit, just as we visited Mexico some summers. It will be great to live there with family and friends who love you. Aren't you excited?" Mamá said, trying to make light of it.

José sank in his chair.

Emilio glanced down, pulled into the well-known dark place again. He could almost hear his twin's thoughts. What about Marco, Pablo, and all his new soccer buddies? Was he supposed to leave the only home he had ever known, the country of his birth? Would he ever become a *fútbol* star if he left America? José had shared his dreams so many times with Emilio. Emilio felt tears running down his cheeks. A tear for his brother. A tear for himself.

José stood up, ready to protest, but then his gaze met Emilio's. Their eyes locked, and Emilio knew José was looking deep into Emilio's soul, seeing the relief, the sorrow, the confusion. José sat down again.

"*Sí*, Mamá," said José flatly. "It will be great moving to Mexico."

When Emilio heard José, he felt like a lead cloud had been lifted. His twin had chosen for both of them. He got up and gave José a warm hug.

Gently, Mamá placed her rosary back in its small wicker box and breathed deeply.

"You know," she said to Papá, "I feel torn about leaving Tony behind. And we don't know if I'll find work in Mexico." She rose, smoothing her shirt, and walked to the stove to finish cleaning.

José had turned Emilio's hug into a wrestling match. They grappled with each other on the floor. Emilio had just pinned José when he saw Mamá clutch the silver medal of the Virgen de Guadalupe that hung by her heart and stare at the sky out the window. For a second, guilt gripped Emilio again, thinking of Mamá's worry, but then José made him laugh, and Mamá turned to them.

A broad smile brightened her face as she looked from Emilio to José and back to Emilio.

"Mis milagros," Mamá whispered.

And suddenly Emilio knew it was their smiles that fed Mamá's. That—*that*—was the miracle.

SELFIE

El que quiera celeste, que le cueste.

"Picture Day!" Marla said to herself, standing in front of the bathroom mirror. She applied a little lip gloss, wanting to look good for Picture Day at school. Marla tilted her head this way and that to check out her new highlights. That's when she noticed it. The ring around the sides of her neck had darkened. It had spread toward the front, too! She cringed. She pulled her hair up and rubbed her neck with soap and water until it felt raw, but the ring remained. Frantic, she headed to the kitchen, stepping over piles of stuff on the floor of the room she shared with Mamá in their East LA apartment. She'd seen on TV that potatoes lightened the skin. She opened the fridge to find it almost empty, the last potato rotten. Marla sighed. It was that time of the month again. Mamá made barely enough for the rent, so they depended on government help for food, and the money always came on the tenth. Today was September 9.

"What are you searching for?" asked Mamá as she retrieved her insulin vial from the refrigerator door and filled a needle with fluid.

"It's my ring," said Marla. "I mean, my neck." Sometimes Marla struggled to say what she meant. "It's getting darker."

Kevin, Marla's younger brother, overheard her from his bed in the living room.

"Marla has a dirty neck! Marla has a dirty neck!" he started chanting gleefully.

"Moron!" Marla screamed, lunging at her brother. She chased him around the apartment and out into the open hall until she got winded.

She steadied herself against the banister of the outdoor stairs. Recovered, she walked back inside.

"Don't pay attention to him," said Mamá as she injected the sharp needle into her stomach with a jab.

The familiar sight sent shivers through Marla. No matter how many times she watched her mother inject herself, Marla couldn't get used to it. She dreaded becoming like Mamá, sick and tired all the time. Mamá lived from insulin shot to insulin shot. Four days a week Mamá would drag herself to the minimum-wage job she had at the nearby cell-phone repair center. Mamá used to be an assistant manager at a moving company, but the job had required such long hours that she'd had to quit. Diabetes tired Mamá. Still, Mamá refused to go on disability. *You have to earn your living,* she would say to Marla all the time.

"Have breakfast, Marla!" Mamá called as Marla was getting ready to leave. Marla grabbed the last bag of potato chips and headed for the school bus stop at the corner of Tim and Eastern.

As she saw the bus approach, Marla turned on her cell phone and swiveled its camera to look at herself on the screen as if it were a mirror. For her thirteenth birthday, a hairdresser friend of her mother's had highlighted her hair. Now Marla swept her hair over her chest. She didn't want her friends Keisha and Tina to notice the ring on her neck.

Marla boarded the bus and found her friends in their usual seats.

"Hey!" Marla said, sliding into the seat in front of her friends. "Love your earrings, Keisha!" she said. Marla liked being friendly.

"And I like your highlights," responded Keisha.

"Thanks," said Marla, running her fingers through her hair. "Hey, look over. Selfie!" Marla snapped a photo of the three of them. She was always taking pictures. She looked at the picture. Neither of her friends had a neck ring. Marla frowned and put her phone away. She remembered her last visit to the doctor. She had gone into the examining room on her own. Mamá had stayed behind to fill out some paperwork. Dr. Lee had examined her skin. The ring had been much fainter then. Still, the doctor had asked many questions. Did she get tired easily? What did she eat at home? Did she avoid sweet drinks? Did she choose healthy meals at school? Did she play sports? Marla had told Dr. Lee that Mamá bought whatever was on sale at the Food 4 Less. Sports were not her thing, but she liked math and social studies. Dr. Lee had explained that the dark pigmentation around her neck was a sign of prediabetes. It meant that Marla was not processing sugars well. Marla remembered Dr. Lee's every word: *You have strong risk factors for type 2 diabetes. You need to make an effort to eat better and exercise. Otherwise you'll become as ill as your mom.* Marla's smile had vanished.

All day at school Marla looked forward to seventh period. She loved her social studies teacher. Ms. García was young and pretty and funny, and she knew so much. She always called on Marla whenever Marla raised her hand. The period was almost over when Ms. García asked if anyone had gone to the 234th birthday of the founding of the city of Los Angeles. Before anyone could answer, the bell rang and all the students stampeded out of the room. Marla felt sorry for Ms. García and stayed behind.

"How was it?" Marla asked, picking up her backpack with one hand and pulling down her tunic with the other.

"You would have loved it, Marla," Ms. García said. "There was a procession of pedestrians and bicyclists that started at the Mission San Gabriel and ended in El Pueblo de Los Angeles. There were reenactments, readings, musical numbers, and food vendors. I even joined the cyclists in the procession," she added as she gathered her things.

"You biked all that way?" asked Marla, arching her eyebrows.

"It's not much of a ride. Just nine miles!" said Ms. García as she walked out of the classroom. "Do you bike, Marla?"

"No. I mean, yes," Marla answered. "Last time I biked I was real little." She looked sideways. "I don't have a bike anymore."

"Maybe one day you can borrow a bike and join one of these events," said Ms. García as she headed toward the parking lot. "You'd like it."

Marla thought that she wouldn't be able to cover nine miles even if she owned a bike. She touched the back of her neck. Watching the teacher weaving gracefully in between the hordes of students running every which way, Marla wished she could be just like Ms. García.

The next day was September 10, and Marla went with Kevin and Mamá to the Food 4 Less in Huntington. It was time to get a month's worth of groceries. Marla always liked shopping for food. The huge warehouse had big aisles lined with items sold in large quantities. Bright lights shone on the food items, and bunches of balloons decorated the displays.

"I'm hungry," whined Kevin as soon as Mamá leaned over her shopping cart to read the store's flyer.

"*¡Ay, niño!*" complained Mamá. "Let me finish checking the sales!" Mamá always tried to stretch the money as much as she could. That often meant buying food that had a long shelf life. Just recently, Mamá had taken a nutrition class, and she was intent on making better food choices. Mamá examined her grocery list to see if anything on it was discounted.

"I'm so hungry," whimpered Kevin. "Please."

Mamá gave up. "Okay. Pick something healthy that's not more than a dollar."

Marla looked at her brother and rolled her eyes. The ten-year-old was such a pain.

After Kevin left, Mamá sent Marla to the produce section to look for a couple of the cantaloupes on sale. She would soon follow, Mamá told Marla.

Spotting the cantaloupe bin, Marla noticed a big, muscular woman standing next to it, browsing through the melons. The woman was wearing a T-shirt from the event Ms. García had been talking about. Curious, Marla thought of a way of making conversation.

"This one's ripe. Yes?" Marla asked, a cantaloupe in her hand.

"Let me help you," said the woman. She smelled Marla's melon. "No. Not yet. They should smell sweet." The woman tested another melon and handed it to Marla. "This one's ready."

"Thank you!" said Marla. "Do you like to bike?" she blurted out. "I'm sorry." Marla giggled. "That's so rude of me. I didn't mean to be nosy. I'm Marla."

"No worries," said the woman. "I'm Emma." Emma told Marla all about the Eastside Bike Club, which she was a member of. "We're like a big family. Want to join?"

"Thanks," said Marla. "But I don't have a bike."

"Well," said Emma, "one of our members has a bike shop and sometimes lets young people ride one of his rental bikes for free."

"Really?" Marla asked. She waved Mamá over as soon as Marla spotted her. Marla eagerly introduced Emma to Mamá, wanting to talk about the club. But after a quick exchange, Mamá excused herself to continue their shopping.

As soon as they had left the produce aisle, Marla started thinking about how great it would be to ride a bike again. She'd fallen in love with biking the first time she rode without Abuelo's steadying hand, back when she was five. Now, years later, to go on her own around Los Angeles would be really, really cool. Marla touched her neck. Maybe the ring would fade.

"Mamá! Can I join Emma's bike club?" Marla squealed once they were far enough away from Emma. "They ride on Tuesday evenings at six thirty, and they'd lend me a bike for free. Free!"

"Marla, ¿estás loca?" asked Mamá. "What has gotten into you? You can't ride at night! And with strangers."

"But Dr. Lee said I needed exercise!" exclaimed

Marla the moment Kevin returned with his mouth orange from eating a whole bag of cheese curls and carrying the opened variety pack under his arm.

"Kevin!" Mamá scolded. "I told you healthy and a dollar or less."

"There's twenty packs for eleven ninety-five," said Kevin. "Cheaper than last month's, and some are cheesy!"

"*¡Ay, niño!*" Mamá nodded in defeat. "I wanted to buy healthy things this time. Now we're stuck with getting the opened pack. Never again. You hear me?"

Marla thumped Kevin on the head. He was grinning as he dropped the package in the cart. Then she placed her hand on Mamá's forearm.

"Let me try the club, pleeease," begged Marla. "I'm thirteen!"

"No, Marla," Mamá insisted. "No."

"What?" fumed Marla, stopping in her tracks. "You want me to be just like you?"

Mamá turned to look at Marla, her gaze tired and sad. Marla glanced away, and for an instant she wished she could take back her words. But she said nothing. The family shopped for the rest of the items on Mamá's list in complete silence.

Marla took a walk during her lunch break the following day. The school felt like a town with its open paths and paved areas between its many buildings. Marla wanted to ride a bike again. She believed that biking was *the* exercise for her. She remembered how Abuelo used to praise her biking skills. Maybe she could still convince Mamá to let her join the club. After just one loop around the cafeteria building, Marla grew tired and sat on the bench by the vegetable garden. A little while later Ms. García came out with an eighth grader to tend to the plants.

"*Hola, Marla,*" Ms. García greeted her. "You're all flushed. Are you okay?"

"Yeah, it's just that I've been walking to get in better shape," said Marla, sweeping her hair to the front of her neck. "I want to join a bike club." Marla told Ms. García about the club's evening rides and how she hoped to convince Mamá to let her join. She didn't say anything about her prediabetes, or her harsh words to Mamá.

"I see," said Ms. García. She looked at the eighth grader and asked him to get her some tools. Then Ms. García sat next to Marla. "You know, maybe there's another way. Have you thought of looking into a bike co-op? Some have work-to-own programs."

"What do you mean?" asked Marla.

"Well," said Ms. García as she removed her garden gloves, "if you'd like to get a bike, you might be able to do volunteer work for it. Then you could ride while it's still light out."

"Oh," said Marla. "That sounds interesting."

A few days later, Marla sat with Tina and Keisha at the library. They were all using the computers. Marla began to look up bike co-ops. Several showed up on the map. The closest was Bike Lab on Figueroa Street. She'd have to take two buses. Maybe she could go check it out after school. Marla told her friends about her plan.

"Hey, want to go with me this afternoon?" asked Marla.

"Yeah," said Keisha. "Oh no. I have a dentist appointment."

"It looks far away," said Tina. "We can't walk there. Did you ask your mom?"

"No," said Marla. "Not yet." Marla bit her lower lip. She hunched over, holding the nape of her neck with both hands. She didn't think Mamá would let her ride two buses to a place she didn't know about. She would have to go without telling Mamá. She looked up the bus schedules. Marla was sure she could arrive home first, so Mamá would never find out.

The bus ride to the co-op that afternoon felt much longer than it actually was. Marla was the first to jump out as soon as the bus got to her stop. She felt butterflies in her stomach as she walked to the shop. It didn't have a sign, but she recognized it by a mural of bikes on the side wall. She turned around to take a selfie in front of the mural. Inside the shop, a thin old man in a cap stood behind the counter. Nearby a couple of young guys tinkered with a bike propped up on a stand. The place was greasy and cluttered. Several bikes hung from wall racks, and Marla wondered if someday one of them would be hers.

"Hi," Marla greeted the old man. "I like your mural."

"Have a bike problem, young lady?" the man asked in a raspy voice.

"Yes," Marla said. "I mean, no. I'd like to work here. To own a bike. It's my teacher. She said you might have a program. You have one?"

"Excuse me?" asked the man as he raised a bushy eyebrow.

Marla hid her giggles with her hand, realizing she hadn't been clear.

"Oh! You mean volunteer," he said. He went on to explain that one of the donated bikes could be hers if she volunteered at least fifteen hours. She had to be thirteen or older, a student, and have parental permission. He then took out a form from under the counter and slid it in front of Marla. Marla thanked him and stared at the bikes hanging from the racks. She itched to get on one. She looked at the form. A parent's signature. She glanced over at the guys covered in tattoos and sighed. She doubted she would ever convince Mamá to let her work here. As she was about to leave, she stopped to examine the flyers of past and upcoming bike rides posted by the doorway. The one Ms. García had gone to was there. *Nine miles,* she thought. She had to convince Mamá. She had to.

Marla rushed home from the bus stop to wait for Mamá at the bottom of the stairs that led to their apartment. She wanted to talk to her in private. Kevin was inside watching TV.

As soon as Marla saw Mamá turn the corner, she jumped to her feet and went to greet her.

"*Hola,* Mami," said Marla. "Give me. I'll carry your things."

"*Hola,*" said Mamá, squinting. "*¿'Mami'?* Something's wrong?"

Marla started to explain the wonderful opportunity she had found. She could buy her own bike by doing volunteer work! Mamá nodded in agreement. Marla told Mamá it would take only fifteen hours, and then she could ride in daylight with her own bike. A little signature was all she needed.

"Where's this place?" asked Mamá as she grabbed on to the railing to walk up the steps.

"Not too far," said Marla. "Figueroa Street."

"That's about forty minutes from here by bus!" said Mamá, turning to look at Marla. "And how did you get this form?"

"It's closer from school," mumbled Marla. "I went right after. Nothing happened." She shrugged and tilted her head.

"*¡Ay!* Marla, Marla." Mamá sighed. "*¿Qué voy a hacer contigo?* What am I going to do with you?"

After much begging, Mamá agreed to go on Saturday to the Bike Lab to check it out.

✳ ✳ ✳

Saturday morning came and Marla couldn't contain herself. She kept describing to Mamá over and over again the bikes she had seen. She told Mamá how she knew this was the exercise for her. If he were alive, Abuelo would be happy. Mamá nodded with a smile. Marla kept talking up the opportunity all the way to the co-op.

After a long chat with the old man, Mr. Ben, Mamá signed the form. Marla would start right then and there and would report to Mamá by text on the hour. She had to be home by four. No excuses. That day Marla did all she was asked. She cleaned the counters. She sorted parts. She learned the names of tools and where to keep them. She buffed two recently donated bikes, one black, one purple, until they were shiny. She reported to Mamá every hour on the dot. Around two o'clock Mr. Ben called her over.

"You've been good," he said. "Tell you what. You can take that one for a ride," he added, pointing to the purple bike.

"Really?" asked Marla. "Thank you, thank you!"

"Just around the block!" he admonished.

With the help of another volunteer Marla took the bike off the rack and grabbed a nearby helmet. She walked it to the doorway and climbed on it. She stumbled once, twice. But then it seemed like her muscles remembered what to do, and she rode around the block. It felt so good, even if she tired after only two loops.

Marla returned to volunteer at the Bike Lab four more times. There she learned about bike mechanics and care and attended a free class on riding in traffic. She jumped at every chance that came up to ride with customers as they tried out bikes before purchasing them. And she began to notice she could ride for longer periods.

One Saturday Mr. Ben called her away from her work in the bike co-op.

"Tell you what, young lady," Mr. Ben said. "You've earned that purple bike you like so much."

Marla stood on the tips of her toes, tightly holding her hands near her smiling face, as she listened to Mr. Ben's every single word. "Take it home today, along with the helmet you always wear. You don't have to come back anymore, but you'll always be welcome at the shop."

"Thank you! Thank you! Thank you! Thank you!" exclaimed Marla as she clapped her hands.

"One last thing before you take off," said Mr. Ben. "Go clean up the old announcements from the wall and find room for the upcoming events, please."

"Sure," Marla said. She grabbed the stack of new flyers and rushed to the wall to clean and spruce it up as best she could. That's when she saw the flyer announcing the perfect ride for her. The Día de los Muertos Bike Ride. It would be a nine-mile ride in honor of the Day of the Dead, ending with a *fiesta* held at the famous Self Help Graphics & Art center in Boyle Heights. Nine miles. Marla was instantly hooked. The ride was on Sunday,

November 1, starting at three p.m. Four weeks away. Mamá should allow her to ride at that hour. She snapped a picture of the announcement. She could already imagine herself flying by, with a fading ring on her neck.

That afternoon, before leaving the co-op on her own bike, Marla went over to Mr. Ben and hugged him. Riding in the bike lane most of the way home, she looked at the birds flying above her. And she felt a kinship with them. As soon as she arrived, she called Mamá and Kevin from the parking lot of their apartment.

Kevin came out first.

"Wow!" he said. "Nifty bike! Can I ride it?"

"Not now," Marla answered.

"Whatever! It's a girl's bike anyway," he added, and headed back inside to watch TV.

"Look at you!" exclaimed Mamá, coming down the steps to get a closer look. "What a great bike you earned yourself!"

Marla told Mamá all about the Día de los

Muertos event and how much she would love to participate.

"Well, if it's during the day and you ride with someone I know, maybe it would be okay," said Mamá. "I'd love to go to the Self Help Graphics fiesta for Day of the Dead. The last time I went I was younger than you!"

"You mean you would actually let me go?" asked Marla. But then she remembered the condition. She needed to ride with someone Mamá knew. She slumped over the handlebars of her bike. "Who am I going to ask?"

"You'll find someone," said Mamá.

The first chance she had, Marla sought out Ms. García.

"Ms. García, thank you!" Marla cried. "I have my own bike!" Marla told Ms. García she had finally finished her volunteer work at the co-op. She told her about Abuelo. She said her dream was to join the Day of the Dead ride on November 1.

Ms. García said she understood and would probably join the ride herself.

Marla got all flustered thinking about the possibility of riding alongside her favorite teacher and, after waving good-bye, left to talk to Keisha and Tina.

"Do you think I can ask her?"

"I don't know," Tina replied as they walked around the school grounds during lunch.

"Of course she should!" exclaimed Keisha. "This is her only chance! It's not like her mom is going to let her ride with one of the cool tattooed guys Marla talks about."

"Hmm," said Marla, biting her lower lip. "I'm not sure I can ask. What if she thinks it's weird? She's a teacher."

On October 23 Ms. García did a unit on the Day of the Dead. Marla listened intently. And as she heard Ms. García's closing words—"It's not about skull candy or dressing up, but about honoring

the dead and remembering we all turn to dust"—
Marla made up her mind. She would ask her
teacher after class. For Abuelo, for herself.

"Ms. García," said Marla. "You know how I
really want to go to the Day of the Dead ride?"

"Yes?" said Ms. García.

"Well . . ." Marla hesitated. "My mom won't let
me go if I don't ride with someone she knows. . . ."
Marla looked down.

"She's right," said Ms. García.

"Yeah," said Marla, her eyes still downcast. "I
know, and . . . ah." Marla bit her lower lip.

"We could ride together," said Ms. García.

Marla couldn't believe her luck! She was going
to actually do the nine-mile ride! And—with her
favorite teacher!

Sunday, November 1, the Day of the Dead, had
finally arrived. Marla slipped into her comfy
black leggings and the black sweatshirt that Keisha and Tina had painted for her with bright

flowers and white skulls. She brushed her hair into a low ponytail that she could wear with her helmet. She filled her water bottle and placed it in its rack on the bike. Ms. García was picking her up at 2:40. It was twelve thirty now, and Marla was stapling marigolds around the border of a collage of photos of Abuelo that she and Mamá had made together. Marla had returned to the Bike Lab a few more times, and Mr. Ben had helped her attach a rack to carry her memorial. She took selfies with the finished memorial, and with Mamá and Kevin and her by the bike. She couldn't wait to be picked up. Then the phone rang. It was Ms. García.

"Hi, Marla," Ms. García said in a serious tone. "I need to talk to your mom, please."

"Sure," said Marla, handing her cell phone to Mamá. Marla started to fidget.

"*Sí, sí.* I understand," said Mamá. "Oh, well. I don't know. Let me think about it. Marla will call you back."

Mamá told Marla that Ms. García had a family emergency and would not be free in time for the ride. She had talked to a friend who could take Ms. García's place.

"Some friend called Emma," Mamá said.

At first Marla slumped. She wouldn't be riding with Ms. García after all. She looked at every photo in Abuelo's memorial. Accomplishing the ride was more important than anything. Emma . . . *Emma*? Marla remembered the woman who had helped her with the melons.

"We've met Emma!" exclaimed Marla. "Way back at the Food 4 Less."

"How do you know it's the same Emma?" asked Mamá.

"Yeah, I don't." Marla sighed, hunching over in defeat. She reached for her water bottle and took a long drink.

"Well," said Mamá, "if Ms. García trusts her to ride with you, and I can talk to Emma before you leave, I guess it's okay."

Then Marla felt the urge to do something she should have done weeks before. She hugged Mamá tight and kissed her on the cheek. "I'm sorry," she whispered. "It was mean. What I said to you at the store."

"It's okay," said Mamá, leaning her head against Marla's. "I love you."

At 2:35 Marla took her decorated bike down the stairs to the parking lot. It turned out that the Emma who came to pick up Marla *was* the same Emma they had met at the grocery store. Mamá chatted with Emma briefly and gave Marla the thumbs-up. Marla blew a kiss to Mamá. She knew she would see Mamá later at the Self Help Graphics party. Mamá didn't want to miss Marla's first big ride and had told her she would be there waiting. Marla set off on her bike, following Emma to the meet-up point in front of the Food 4 Less.

There were about forty people waiting when Marla and Emma arrived. People chatted with one another. Marla pulled out her phone and shot many pictures of the bikers' decorations and outfits. She met a few of Emma's friends before they all took off for the Parque de Mexico six miles away. There another cycling club would join them for the remainder of the distance.

The first couple of miles were hard. Marla worried that she wouldn't be able to keep up with the group's pace down Huntington Drive. But then she noticed that whenever she fell behind, Emma or one of Emma's friends cycled back to encourage Marla. That made her feel better. For the next few miles Marla was able to ride smoothly. She loved the feeling of riding with a bunch of people, of being part of something bigger than herself. She felt both free and totally embraced. She was in the middle of the pack when they got to the park. There was a blur of bicyclists waiting, maybe a hundred. Marla was tired and hoped they would rest a bit. But the club leaders stopped only long enough to greet one another and continued on. They needed to get to the Mariachi Plaza in time to join the Day of the Dead procession at five o'clock.

Marla rode right behind Emma, trying not to lose sight of her. Pedaling up a slight hill, Marla felt too out of breath. Her mouth was dry. She had never biked this distance all at once. How much more to the plaza? She stopped to rest and drink water. When Marla looked up, Emma had blended into the pack. Riders kept swishing by. Marla panicked. She didn't want to be left behind. She rose up to pedal harder and get ahead just as the pack was making the turn onto Gallardo Street. When she turned, she hit the curb. She lost her balance and fell off her bike.

A cute boy from the other club stopped. "Are you okay?" he asked.

Marla felt dizzy. "It's okay; I just scraped my hands," she lied, embarrassed.

Soon Marla heard Emma calling, "What happened?"

"I'm okay," Marla said, getting back on the bike.

She felt weak and shaken after the fall, but she had worked too hard not to accomplish this ride. So she willed away her fear of failing by thinking of Abuelo's steadying hand.

They rode into the Mariachi Plaza a little before five. Hundreds of people were in *calacas* and *calaveras* costumes. The skeletons and skulls mocking and honoring death packed the square, spilling onto Bailey Street. Marla was scanning the crowd for Mamá when she felt someone pinch her side.

"Gotcha!" said Kevin, his face painted white with large black circles for eyes and black stitches across his mouth. She punched him lightly in his stomach, glad to see him. Keisha and Tina came right behind Kevin, wearing face paint over half of their faces. It was unique.

"Oh, I want my face painted just like that!" Marla exclaimed, wiping sweat off her face with the small square of terry cloth Mamá had given her for good luck.

"The best face painters are at the art center," said Tina.

"Yeah, but we couldn't wait," added Keisha.

Soon Mamá appeared, walking alongside Ms. García, who waved to Emma.

"Mamá, Mamá! I did it!" Marla called.

"*¡Felicidades!*" Mamá exclaimed as she got closer. "I knew you would!"

"You should be proud of yourself," said Ms. García. "I'm glad I was able to take care of things on time to see you at the finish line."

"Thank you," Marla said. She felt herself blush a little and turned to join Keisha and Tina, who had bumped into someone from school. As she left, Marla overheard Mamá thanking Emma for riding with her. She also heard Ms. García tell Mamá what a great daughter she had. Marla felt warm inside. All her favorite people had come to see her finish her first big ride.

In the short procession afterward, Marla walked her bike alongside Mamá, Kevin, Keisha, and Tina. They arrived at the Self Help Graphics & Art event to find people in Aztec costumes and huge papier-mâché masks. There were *calaveras* everywhere: painted on people's faces and clothing, carved into jewelry and candy. In the center's galleries, the altars to departed loved ones were lit by candlelight and covered in brilliant orange marigolds. Outside, people danced to live music.

Tina and Keisha found a face-painting booth for Marla, and she had her face painted by a true artist. He painted one half white, her eye with black eye shadow at the center of a big red heart outlined with sparkling jewels. Her mouth became a black wavy line stitched across and curling at the cheek. The other half of her face was made to look like Frida Kahlo's. He finished by crowning her head with red paper flowers.

"I look beautiful!" Marla exclaimed when she looked at herself in the camera of her phone. Then she took a group selfie with Mamá and Kevin and Keisha and Tina all surrounding Abuelo's collage.

On Monday, Marla got up extra early to wash off any leftover makeup from the night before. And as she dried herself, Marla tilted her head in front of the bathroom mirror and looked at her clean, glowing face. That's when she noticed it. The ring around her neck was gone.

Marla smiled wide, proud and strong.

GÜERA

Las apariencias engañan.

Ta-ra-ta-ra-ta-ra-ta-ra . . .

I rush for the Brook Avenue station to catch the
6 train to Brooklyn Bridge. I need to get on it by
five thirty or I'm gonna be late! I'm meeting Cousin
Tita at La Casa Azul on 103rd Street for my song-
writing class. Just five stops. Ten minutes and I'll
be there. I run down the stairs, pulling up my long
curls with all my fingers into a tight *colita*. Tying
the ponytail up quick with the rubber band on my
wrist. Plaid bag across my shoulders, cell in the

pocket of my tight new jeans. Oops! It's vibrating. Must look. I stop in my tracks, right in the middle of the stairs, to take out my iPhone, just like I know I should never do. It's annoying . . . I get it. But I *have* to see! A text: *#coolfiesta*! Instagram link. Yeah! Pictures from this weekend's party at Auntie Angie's house. Tapping fast I find—*La Familia*.

Laughs are coming from behind: Someone bumps into me; I almost stumble and catch my plaid bag. "Hey, keep moving!" a man in a suit screams as he zooms past me, briefcase in hand. I know, I know! I wiggle the phone back into my pants, slide out the MetroCard, zip through the turnstile. I show up at the southbound platform at the same time as the chrome-y train. Walk in right behind an army man. Makes me feel safe. Don't know why. The train swallows all of us up in its sticky hot summer mess. In the corner a woman clips her toenails. Disgusting. I hold on to a pole. At 5:31, first stop, two guys get in. One is a *chaparro*, a shorty. I've seen the other one—he's wearing a muscle shirt and gold chain. From Mott Haven High? Kind of cute. Behind me, an old man gets up. I slide into his seat, peer at my phone to check—*La Familia*.

There they are: Rita, Tita, Clara, Laura, Guada, Mari, Fabio, Artur, Ana, and me. All the cousins on top of each other, laughing, teasing, elbowing, fighting for the front spots. Tall, short, heavy, thin, older, younger, shy, and bold. All of them with skin the color of Auntie Angie's craved-by-all-cousins hot chocolate, tinged with cinnamon, spiced with chili.

Cho-co-cho-co-con-ají . . .

All belong—but me. Me sticking out like a sore thumb. Me with peaches-and-cream legs, like ghost legs next to Rita's. Me with copper hair, like bleached-from-the-sun hair next to Mari's jet-black-like-*azabache* hair. Mari would give anything for my hair, she says. I roll my eyes when I hear that. I want to change places with her so bad! And Guada wraps her ivory scarf around my arm just to show that her scarf and my skin are the same shade. Artur jokes that I was found in a trash can, and that's why I'm so different. And that makes Fabio bend over laughing. But Tita gets all worked up and sticks up for me: "Don't bother Güera!" *Sí*, I'm Güera for all nine cousins, Güerita for *tíos* and *abuelos*. *La Familia* say it's just *de cariño* they call me that way. 'Cause they love me so. I'm the blonde one; I'm the *güera*. When strangers ask my name, I answer Vicky, my given name. But who am I, Vicky or Güera?

Cho-co-cho-co-cho-co-güe-ra . . . I have a new song dancing in my head.

At 125th Street I can feel someone staring. It's just that subway sense. I look up. Muscle guy and the *chaparro* are now standing close. Too close. I put my earbuds on. Muscle guy fixes his hair, flexes his muscles. Oh, God—not so cute anymore. The *chaparro* fakes a cough. They see me looking and glance away like they're wanting to hide something. But I see them. I stare at my phone and turn off my music. I'm listening to what they say. They talk in fast Spanish. They don't whisper, because they figure it's some secret language I don't understand. But I do.

"A que no se da cuenta la güerita," says muscle guy. "She won't notice. Go talk to her. *Vé, charla.*"

Why do they want to talk to me now? Creepy. I glance at the LED display sign inside the train. We're at 116th Street. The *chaparro* meets my eyes and smiles a crooked smile. He leans toward the other guy and mutters, *"Tú se lo quitas."* My ears perk up. They want to steal something from me. But what? Chimes. It's a text from Tita, who's already at the bookstore. Can't wait for me to be there. And then I know. My phone! That's what they want. I check and see the army guy is right across from me. The doors open for 110th Street. The woman on my left gets up, and the *chaparro* eases into her seat. Gross. I inch away from him. His nasty cologne invades my space. I keep my cool.

"Hey," he says to me. "I'm JT. You?"

I feel my temperature rising, like these two are dumb enough to think I'll fall for it. How annoying. The voice on the loudspeaker announces 103rd Street. My stop! But I stay put. Don't leave my seat yet. Wait until the doors are just about to close.

Now.

I slide my cell in my bag. I dash to the exit. The doors creak to close. Just before stepping out, I turn, stare down the sleazy guys, and say,

"My name is Güera. And I understood *cada palabra.*"

Their jaws drop. Like this girl with skin the color of hot white chocolate doesn't belong. But I do—I have chili too.

I run up the stairs and into East Harlem.

Cho-co-cho-co-cho-co-DUL-ce

Cho-co-cho-co-cho-co-SWEET

Cho-co-cho-co-cho-co-GÜE-ra

Cho-co-chi-ca-con-a-JÍ

BURRITO MAN

Nadie sabe el bien que tiene hasta que lo pierde.

I stood once again at the corner of Seventeenth and K in downtown Washington, DC, Papi's corner. This time I was alone. I knelt down to lean the sign against the tall elm and licked a salty tear running down my cheek.

A flock of sparrows swirled above me, triggering a rush of memories from years ago . . .

"M'hijita." I hear my father calling, sounding as close as if he were next to me. "Come down already,

I'm going to be late for work!"

I wash my sleepiness away with a splash of cold water. It's four in the morning. Today is Take Your Child to Work Day. I don't want to go. If only I could have gotten out of it. I wish I were Tania. Her dad is a doctor's tech. Or Marisa. Hers is a big-time lawyer, so she'll probably get to spend the day swiveling in a plush leather chair in an air-conditioned office. Even Mami works in an office. She's a school secretary. Not Papi, though. He's just a food-cart vendor. He sells burritos. I'll be stuck standing at the corner of Seventeenth and K, all day, in the traffic and hot sun. At least none of my friends will see me.

By the time we pull into the downtown ware-house parking lot, birds are chirping—soft chirps that grow into a full-blown chorus. Nature wakes up. Not me, not yet. I yawn big, and the clanking noises Papi makes hooking the burrito cart to his old rusty truck shake me up. He slides back in, and we rumble down the street to his assigned corner.

"Alex," he says to me. "*Por favor*, take the sauces and condiments out of the box and set them up there."

"Okay, okay," I mumble as I sweep back the long strand of hair blocking my vision. I take my time lining up the jars and bottles on the counter in the shade of the cart's green-and-white-striped awning.

"It's going to be a great day with you here!" Papi adds.

"Really?" I ask, raising my eyebrows.

"*Sí, sí, m'hijita, ya verás,*" he says. "You'll see." He starts to whistle his favorite folk song from El Salvador. And I force myself to remember why I am here instead of chatting with my friends on the school bus. At the back-to-school night, Ms. Chu encouraged parents to take their kids to work today. And Papi liked the idea. *Really* liked it. I tried to get out of it and said I should go with Mami instead. No luck.

Papi turns on the propane gas and starts to simmer the vats of beans. Black beans, pinto beans, and *refritos.* No meat. Meat is too expensive and sometimes spoils, Papi says. Beans are better. And rice. And cheese. And guacamole. I like my burrito with meat, though.

And there's coffee. Papi offers lots of it—espresso, cappuccino, and, lately, what a Cuban *fútbol* friend of his taught him to make: *cortadito.* For that you cut the black espresso with a drop of milk. Now that I'm twelve, Papi puts me in charge of the coffee. I'm old enough, he says.

It's only half past six, and out of a tall building comes a man in a classy suit and tie making a bee-line for our stand. The first customer. He's looking straight at the coffee, though. Am I ready to serve him? I panic.

"Good morning, Mr. Wallace!" My father greets him with a broad smile. "The usual?"

"*Buenos días*, Miguel," the man responds in a deep voice. "Yes, please."

"Black coffee, two sugars, Alex," Papi says.

A simple order—I smile, relieved. The man and

Papi begin to chat loudly about last night's basketball game, and that gives me lots of time to get
the coffee ready. Papi asks about his kids by name.
I perk up my ears and wonder how is it that Papi
knows so much about those kids. The man's grin
gets wider with each one of my father's comments.

"So who is this lovely young lady?" the man
asks, reaching for his fresh coffee.

"*Ahh*, this is Alex. She's my special helper. Her
first time here!" Papi says. "She's a good student,
you know. I told you she's going to college one day,
right?"

The man looks at me like he's seeing a movie
star or something.

"So this is the famous Alex!" he finally says,
extending his hand to shake mine. "I'm delighted
to meet you."

The word *famous* makes my ears burn, so I'm
quick to shake the man's hand and look away. My
gaze lands on the pink-wrapped tin next to Papi's
honor-system coffee-payment jar. I frown when I

notice the handwritten sign on the tin. *Alex's College Fund*, it reads. My mind races, trying to think of a way to hide the sign.

"I'll be sure to tell everyone at the office to come to Miguel's corner and finally meet Alex," the man says, dropping payment for his coffee in the honor-system jar. I'm about to slide the pink tin behind some bottles when the man slips a dollar into it.

His gesture makes my eyes go wide and my jaw drop. I gasp. I long to be invisible.

The morning turns to noon, and the line for Miguel's Burritos now curves around the corner. Papi fills warm spinach and corn tortillas with beans and rice and sauces to order, and neatly wraps the burritos in tinfoil. They do smell good. Funny how he seems to know so many of his customers, and most everyone has heard of me. The novelty of being today's main attraction begins to wear off. One gets used to being a celebrity, you know. I simply smile and hand out hot and cold drinks. Just when I feel kind of tired of standing up and being polite, Papi pats me gently on the back.

"Take a break, Alex," he says. "Here's your favorite, *tu favorito*." He hands me a fat burrito filled with pinto beans, melted cheese, and his special spicy guacamole. It's *sooo* delicious I don't even miss the meat. Papi is humming his tune again. I look at him and smile a little smile. I imagine Marisa in the plush chair of her dad's fancy office and think maybe I don't want to trade with her anymore.

"Have a great evening!" Papi waves to the last customer hours later. "*¡Hasta mañana!*"

By the time we drive back home, it's already dark.

"Papi?" I ask. "When are you opening the restaurant you and Mami talk about all the time?"

"One day, Alex, one day," he answers. "It's true that we have some money now. But my customers love me, you know. They'd miss me if I left. I'll think about the restaurant after I finish saving money for your college."

"*Ay, sí*, about that college fund," I say. "You know that pink tin—"

"You like it, right?" Papi asks. "It makes me think of you all day, Alex. The day you go to college will be the greatest day for the whole family!"

"But Papi, that's like in a million years!" I whine.

"And I'll be so proud of you!" Papi exclaims. "What were you saying about the tin?"

I'm about to ask Papi to get rid of it, but instead I lean my head on his shoulder and say, "Oh, never mind."

* * *

The sound of someone's sniffles broke the spell I was in. I turned around to see about a dozen people walking toward me.

It wasn't the eleven-hour work days, the three-hour commute to work, or the endless Sunday afternoons cooking the week's beans that did him in. It had happened suddenly the day before, during one of his league's soccer games. I was there cheering him on. Papi complained of chest pain, and by the time we arrived at the hospital it was *demasiado tarde.* Too late. Mami was in shock. And it fell on me to tell everyone at his workplace about the heart attack. But "everyone at his workplace" meant his downtown customers. So I ended up announcing Papi's death with the hand-painted sign I spent all night making when I couldn't sleep. Men in suits and women with brief-cases, eager for their usual cup of coffee on their way to work, looked puzzled and shaken. A lone homeless man came over and shook his head. I got up and stepped back, letting the strangers get closer. A few of them hugged one another in their shared sorrow.

"Oh my God!" cried a large woman. She stopped in her tracks, took out her cell, and called someone. Minutes later a group of office workers hurried

out of their dark glass building to join her. One of
them bent over to place the bouquet of fresh dahl-
ias she had just purchased at the foot of the sign.

"He was such an upbeat man," she said. "We
often chatted for the whole fifteen minutes of my
coffee break."

"He gave me warm lunch on cold days," said the
homeless man. "Always bragging about that smart
daughter of his."

"I sure hope she'll go to college one day!" agreed
a well-dressed man with a deep voice. "Miguel
was saving toward that for the seventeen years
I've been buying his burritos."

The man didn't notice me. It was Mr. Wallace.
I blinked away my tears as I walked away from
Papi's corner. I thought of the pink tin and smiled.

It has a place of honor in my room now.

"*Sí*. The daughter will go to college next fall," I
whispered.

BAND-AID

No se puede tapar el cielo con la mano.

Alina sat at the picnic table in the cool shade of the banyan tree, with ten of her classmates from parochial school. She had just blown out the twelve candles atop the *tres leches* and strawberry cake, her laugh chiming like silver bells above the applause of her friends, when the phone rang.

"*¿Aló?*" Mami answered, after swallowing a mouthful of the custardy cake. By the tone in Mami's voice, Alina knew it was Papá. Lifting a sliced strawberry as red as her manicured nails,

Mami fed it to Martin, Alina's little brother. He was busy crinkling the bright wrapping paper Alina had teased him with.

"*Gracias* for the cake, *mi amor*. The girls love it!" Mami raved. "Even the baby likes it. I can feel tiny kicks inside me!"

Papá was finishing a concrete patio on this Saturday afternoon and had told Alina he would be home before her party was over. Concrete was what everyone wanted for their patios and driveways in Homestead, Florida. Papá's business was going so well that two years ago they had moved into a bigger house, where Alina, being the only girl, had her own room. Alina loved choosing the fabric for her window curtains. She had helped Mami sew the panels, making sure the pink-and-purple flower pattern aligned perfectly. Since her brothers, Angel and Martin, shared a room, Alina knew her baby sister would move in with her one day. She liked that idea. "I can't wait for *mi hermanita* to be born!" she remembered telling Mami while they were sewing together. "I saw this cute hairdo for baby girls—all you need is pink ribbon and soap and scissors, and you glue little bows to small bunches of the baby's hair with soap. It works, too!" Mami had raised her eyebrows and snorted. "Your sister hasn't been born yet and you're thinking about hairdos?" She had cradled Alina's chin in her soft palm for a moment before returning to her sewing machine.

After a long pause in the phone conversation, Alina saw Mami's smile vanish. Mami ambled back into the house, sliding the patio door closed behind her. When she came out again, Alina's best friend, Jenny, ran up to her.

"Mrs. González," Jenny exclaimed with a little bounce. "Alina loves the matching T-shirts I gave her and the baby. Show your mom, Alina!"

Alina held up the hot pink T-shirts with glittering bird designs. When she peeked from behind them, she noticed Mami's forced smile.

"*Lindas* . . . pretty," Mami said, her voice flat, her gaze lost somewhere beyond the shirts. Alina eyed Mami's face for a moment, but she was soon distracted by her friends' giggles and presents.

Almost a year later, on a humid Friday morning, Alina sat on a faded blue plastic chair just outside the small apartment they now lived in on the other side of the Busway. She was trying to stay cool in a sliver of shadow in the parched yard. In her lap was baby Sofi. Alina needed to feed her something, and she rose to mash a piece of the overripe banana left on the worn kitchen counter, which stayed sticky no matter how many times she, or Mami, cleaned it. She also needed to check on Martin. At six years old, he was still slow to get dressed. Mami had already left for work, and it was up to Alina to make sure her brothers got to school. After that, she had to drop Sofi at the neighbors' before heading to her public middle school.

Things had gotten tough since Papá was no longer with them. The day after her twelfth birthday party, the life she'd always known began to fade away. While still in private school, Alina kept telling her friends that her dad was on a business trip. She added new details every time she retold the story, until it became so real to her that she almost believed it and began to act as if nothing was wrong in front of others. It helped that, at first, Mami didn't talk about what had happened either, waiting for the impossible to occur. Just three weeks after the incident, Sofi was born, and Mami put Alina in charge of her two younger brothers.

Then Alina told Jenny that Papi had extended his business trip. When Mami started to work long hours to make ends meet, Alina told Jenny that Mami wanted to better herself and was taking a course. Each new responsibility that Mami gave Alina cemented Alina's feeling of living temporarily in another girl's body. It was as if the carefree, joyful Alina was simply visiting inside the girl who was burdened with responsibilities. This kind of crazy thinking brought her comfort.

In the middle of July, when Mami announced they could no longer pay the rent and they would soon have to move out of the big house, Alina froze. She didn't know what to tell Jenny. Alina had shared everything with Jenny: her crushes, her fears, her dreams. They had been best friends since the moment they found out they shared the exact same birthday. When she tried to talk to Mami about how to handle things with Jenny, Mami was too tired to talk. So Alina gave up and decided to avoid her friend altogether. Over the next few weeks Jenny texted and called, but Alina didn't answer. But one afternoon Jenny showed up when Alina was packing her things. It was only then that Jenny pried the truth out of her. All of it. "Alina, things can't get any worse for you," she had said. "You've hit bottom; there's nowhere else to go but up!" Alina felt stabbed by these words, robbed of her fantasy, and ashamed. "You don't understand; this never would have happened to you!" Alina replied, wiping the tears that had gathered in her eyes. Jenny knew the truth, and Alina didn't want to face it. It was easier to think that none of it had happened to her, but rather to this other girl, the one who had to do so many chores at home.

Alina wiped Sofi's hands and face after her sister had finished. She filled the sippy cup with tap water.

"Good girl, Sofi, good girl," she said, pressing her lips to Sofi's chubby cheek and placing her in the stroller.

"Hurry up, Martin!" Alina called. "You'll be late for the bus!"

Angel was outside horsing around with the kid next door as he waited for Martin to come out. Boys' shirts and socks were scattered about in the small apartment. Alina groaned, bending over to pick each item up to add to the heap already on the couch. She recognized some of the Goodwill clothes Doña Sánchez had given them, and her brow furrowed. This woman from Nicaragua had visited Alina's family several times. She always brought food collected through her foundation. With each visit Mami rehashed the incident and its consequences. Alina would always leave the room. She had recently learned why Doña Sánchez was called *la gran madre*. The reason made her edgy.

Once the boys were gone, Alina drank a glass of watered-down juice, brushed Sofi's curls, and left the apartment. The counselor had set up a meeting with her today, and Alina wondered what it was about. Months into her first year in public school, she was still trying to learn how it all worked. She blew a final kiss to Sofi, now in the arms of her neighbor, and headed to the bus stop.

At school, she didn't greet anyone in the crowded hallway. She avoided making friends. It was painful to have a best friend and then not have one.

She remembered the last time she had spoken to Jenny. Then Jenny had left message after message on Alina's cell until Alina's phone service was canceled. Now they were no longer neighbors and went to different schools. Still, sometimes things reminded her of Jenny. Like the hot pink T-shirts. And she missed the good times: coordinating outfits, being silly, and most of all, playing soccer with Papi. Thinking of Jenny's ability to kick the ball far over the neighbors' fence, to Papi's delight, brought a smile to Alina's lips.

She opened the door to the counselor's office and greeted Mrs. Park.

"Good morning, Alina," Mrs. Park said. "Please, sit down. I wanted to tell you about a program."

"Yes?" Alina said, tucking stray hair behind her ear.

"It's for free and reduced meals. Your mom told me how hard things are at home."

"What do you mean?" Alina's body became rigid.

The counselor shifted in her chair. "Well, since

your dad was deported . . . ," she said with caution.

Alina crossed her arms. She clenched her fists. "No, he's on a long trip. And he's going to come back. He will!" she exclaimed.

"Alina, please—you'll feel better if you talk about this."

"I don't want to talk about it!" Alina shouted as she stood up, rattling the chair behind her. "You don't understand."

As she closed the door, the memories of that birthday afternoon rushed back. They were unstoppable, like her tears.

"Ay, Diosito santo," Mami had said after the girls left. She had sat next to Alina on the picnic-table bench amid the wrapping paper, the ribbons, the gifts. "Oh my God. Your father. He was pulled over by the police on his way home because the van's registration was expired. They took him into custody. And then they called *la migra.*"

Immigration, Alina thought. A thought that

completely silenced Mami's words, giving way to the numbness that drained all the joy she had been filled with moments before. In this void grew a knot in her stomach and an ache in her heart. That was the beginning of the crazy thinking, where she imagined herself in some sort of nightmare from which she would wake up one day. But eleven months later she still hadn't, and reality started to sink in as she walked the empty hallways back to her classroom.

Alina was in such a daze the remainder of her school day that she missed the school bus and had to walk back home the seven long blocks. At every corner she saw something that reminded her of her dad and the big void he had left. There was the hardware store where he sometimes picked up day laborers. There was the copy place where Alina and Papi printed flyers to promote his business, which she and Jenny distributed around the neighborhood. As she reached Rita's Bakery, Alina stopped at the sight of the *tres leches* cake displayed in the window. The corners of her mouth dropped. And the numbness returned.

Ahead of her she saw the long shadows of the buildings and knew it was later than usual. She was going to be late to pick up Sofi. It wouldn't be the first time, either. Maybe Mami would be late getting home and wouldn't notice.

Upon approaching the apartment building, Alina crossed paths with Doña Sánchez, who waved at her from her car before turning onto the main road. She saw Mami in the distance, seated on the steps outside their apartment with Sofi on her lap, busy chatting with a short woman Alina had not seen before. Sofi wriggled down from Mami's arms and chased after a sparrow hopping on the grass. After a few steps Sofi stumbled and fell to the ground, giggling and clapping her little hands. Alina joined Sofi and caught part of the conversation between Mami and the other woman.

"I'm giving *la gran madre* guardianship. I trust her," said the woman. "Next Saturday at the ranch. There's a notary, too. Since my husband was deported and two of my friends at work were detained by *la migra*, I've been worried sick. My kids are citizens; they have a real chance. If I'm deported they can still stay here living with my cousins with Doña Sánchez as the legal guardian."

"*Sí, sí, entiendo.*" Mami nodded, her eyebrows drawn together in concern. "I understand; it's like what happened to us. *Hola*, Alina," Mami greeted her. "Please, put away the things our friend Doña Sánchez brought." Mami leaned closer to the woman, engrossed in her story.

Alina glared at Mami, lifted her little sister up, and went inside.

In the evening after the boys and Sofi were asleep, Mami grabbed Alina by the arm. "We need to talk," Mami said, her worn hands sorting the laundry from the Laundromat. "Next Saturday we are going to *la gran madre*'s barbecue. I think we need her help. But I wanted to talk to you about it first."

Alina knew what Mami was going to say but

couldn't wrap her thoughts around it. She knew why this woman from Nicaragua was called *la gran madre*. Many parents with American children, who had entered illegally and feared deportation, sought her help. Doña Sánchez had become the legal guardian of more than eight hundred young American citizens. People said she did it because kind strangers had helped her when she arrived, at seventeen, seeking refuge herself. To Alina it seemed impossible to be able to take care of so many children. Alina knew how hard it was to care for only three.

"I'm thinking of granting custody to Doña Sánchez," Mami continued, slumping on the sofa with a wrinkled shirt on her lap.

"Why are you saying that? Am I not good enough help for you?" Alina blurted out, sitting next to Mami. "Is it because sometimes I pick up Sofi late?"

"Like today. But no, *linda*, no," Mami said, reaching for Alina's chin. "It's not that." She tilted her head down. "I'm afraid I could be detained and deported, and you kids would be split up in foster care. I've heard horrible stories about that."

"If you're deported, we'll go with you," pleaded Alina. "We're not splitting up. We could even join Papi in Honduras," she added, trying to lighten her fear with hope.

"You don't know what you're saying." Mami shook her head, rubbing her temples with both hands. "Gangs rule the streets in San Pedro Sula. I can't do that to all of you."

That night Alina couldn't sleep. She thought that if Mami gave Doña Sánchez custody, it might make Mami less afraid of being caught by *la migra*. And if Mami was deported, how was Alina going to provide for her siblings? Was it true that they could all get split up and handed over to different foster families? She could not imagine being apart from her brothers and sister. Maybe if she were a better helper to Mami, Mami wouldn't think of granting custody to Doña Sánchez. Alina was scared. And fear forced Alina to peek out of the fog in which she lived. This was her life. And it sucked. She missed talking to Jenny.

All week Alina was on time to pick up Sofi. She did extra chores at home. She mopped the kitchen floor, started dinner, and helped her brothers with homework, so Mami returned from work to find everything in order. On Thursday Alina found three dollars deep inside one of the pockets of her backpack and decided to buy cans of beans and coconut milk at the dollar store to make *resanbinsi*. Alina hoped that the special rice-and-beans dish would help convince Mami not to go to the Saturday event.

Friday afternoon when she went to pick up Sofi, the neighbor gave Alina some cilantro and garlic for her dish. At home, with Sofi playing inside an empty old box from the move, Alina started chopping onions and garlic, and measuring rice, water, and salt. She could barely concentrate: Her mind kept jumping from images of her dad in a crime-ridden country she didn't know, to Mami's foreboding words, to what a foster family might look like. With all the chatter in her brain she didn't hear the doorbell ring.

"Alina!" someone called, knocking on the front door. Alina immediately recognized the voice. It was Jenny.

"I've missed you, girl!" Jenny said, hugging Alina tight the moment the door swung open.

"What are you doing here?" asked Alina. "And how did you find out where I lived?"

"I asked the Sisters at school, silly," said Jenny. "They know we're best friends. It's been too long. And with our birthday coming up on Monday I wanted to see you! So I convinced my mom to drop me here for an hour while she runs some errands. Here, this is for you."

Alina waved at Jenny's mom as she backed out of the parking space. She looked at the birthday card in her hands and lifted her gaze to meet Jenny's eyes. She smiled. Yes. It had been way too long. She pulled Jenny inside the apartment and crumpled on the sofa, tired and relieved at the same time. It was as though the months of silence between them had disappeared. The stories poured out of Alina. Alina told Jenny about public school, and life without Papi, about Doña Sánchez, and Mami's words. And while both of them played with Sofi, Alina even told Jenny how she hoped her special meal would change Mami's mind.

"Wow, I don't know what to say," Jenny whispered. "The whole thing sucks." She hugged Alina again.

"I wanted so much to believe this was not happening to me," Alina said.

"I would have felt the same way," said Jenny. "Really. I hope your plan works. Hey, want me to help set the table?"

When dinnertime came, Alina mentioned Jenny's visit to Mami. She described how they had decorated the rice dish together before her brothers arrived home from elementary school. Angel and Martin liked her *resanbinsi* so much that they scraped up all the bits of rice stuck to the bottom of the pot. Sofi smiled at each black bean she picked up and placed in her mouth.

"*Gracias*, Alina, you made a delicious dinner," Mami said. She looked content.

"So . . . can we skip tomorrow's event?" Alina asked hopefully, her plate untouched.

"*Ay, linda,*" Mami said. "Is that what all this was about?"

"No. I mean yes," said Alina, on the edge of her seat. "What are we going to do?"

"We are still going, Alina." Mami sighed. "Eat your dinner. You barely eat anymore," Mami added as she picked up the dishes.

"I'm not hungry," said Alina, feeling like a pierced balloon slowly shrinking. "I'll get Sofi ready for bed."

❋ ❋ ❋

The next day a volunteer from Doña Sánchez's foundation showed up in a van early in the morning to take them to *la gran madre*'s barbecue at her ranch house. On the highway Alina stared out the window listlessly, halfway wishing something would happen so they would never reach their destination.

Doña Sánchez's ranch was beautiful. After they all greeted *la gran madre*, Alina's brothers ran toward a rope swing. For a moment Alina stood there, overwhelmed by the sounds, sights, and smells of the party. The backyard was dotted with white folding chairs next to long tables dressed in pink plastic tablecloths. Blue, pink, and yellow balloons swayed in the breeze around the huge orange deck. A donkey piñata dangled from the basketball hoop. Farther out along a row of trees, a line of excited kids waited their turn for cotton candy. There were kids sharing the contents of their goody bags, playing with hula hoops, dancing to the salsa music, and racing one another.

Alina felt like her surroundings were at odds with her feelings. And she wished for this woman to be less kind, less generous and welcoming.

"Go make friends, Alina," Mami suggested, taking Sofi in her arms and walking toward a woman she seemed to know. Looking around, Alina was sure that most of the 150 kids scattered about were American citizens like her. Torn apart from a mom, or dad, or both. Her gaze settled on the short woman Mami was talking with and she recognized her as the one who would grant custody of her own children today. And the familiar knot in Alina's stomach tightened.

Right after lunch Doña Sánchez gathered the adults on the deck. She waved a white form in the air and asked for those who were interested in her guardianship to follow her inside the house. Mami gathered her children. Alina felt her hands go clammy and held Sofi in her arms before stepping in.

Two other families were seated in the living

room. When it was Alina's family's turn, they walked into the dining room in silence. Mami sat across from Doña Sánchez and a man. There were legal forms in English that Alina knew Mami could not understand. Mami kept saying the names of her children so Doña Sánchez could learn them: Alina, Angel, Martin, Sofi.

Then the man explained in Spanish what the legal paper meant and slid the form toward Mami along with a pen. Mami took the pen and turned to look at each of her children: Sofi, Martin, Angel, Alina. Alina locked eyes with Mami and felt Mami's gaze melting her heart. It was as if Mami had spoken a thousand beautiful words to her without ever opening her mouth. Mami turned and slid the paper back to the man.

"I'm not ready," she said.

And something broke loose within Alina; she felt like birds were tickling her insides. She looked up and laughed.

Her laugh chiming like silver bells, once again.

an centuries-old cult practice. Studen
ot only learn about human rights defen
rs, but they also are trained to becor
efenders themselves.

Following the implementation of STT
ccording to a forthcoming independen
study we commissioned, Bucyrus students
eported a change in attitude regarding
ullying, particularly their awarenes
ullying as an issue. Administrators
een an increase in reports of
ne student described the SITP
s "helpful not just in handli
ut [providing] reason to
inded about other peop

We went to Bucyrus to
o Power, our first
irectly with a sch
arget bull
urselves
ights violation. I
oweress the
s is a threat
ducation fr rom p
s the first human ri
f students in
onfront. As a
s not somet
Two chi
merica?
ay of scho
nsafe. Loo
ot afford
mply sta
egislation h
istrict of Co

But laws
nough. We mu
aving the syste
ullying. We mu
deals of civility a
reate environmen
verywhere our
lay.

Putting prev
revention is th
ewly launched ec
afe Environments achiev
ving prevention, Engagem
nd Teaching respect. Th
ides resources for paren
ommunity members to
nvironments through a human
ramework that instills responsibi
pect and resiliency to prevent bull

The initiative's name is our ans
ritics who say bullying is ingrain
ulture of an American childhoo
eople, I ask: Who remembe
hen wearing a seat belt w
ptional?

In my father's lifetime,
eren't even required to ins
their vehicles, and it wasn't
at riders were required to use
hen my daughters get in a ca
utting on their seat belts is second
just one generation, we watc
rofound shift in social norms relat
eat belts. How many people in 1984 sa
at Americans would never be persuad
o change an ingrained behavior in th
ame of public safety?

We can change for the better. We do it
e time, and our children are even bet
t it than we are. Parents, teachers, neigh

FIRSTBORN

Hay que coger al toro por los cuernos.

My older sister, Brígida, hated the move. We came to Florida from Puerto Rico last summer after my mother decided she had had enough of the *locura* of the island.

The last craziness happened when Mami was out on our front porch talking to the neighbor, and two thugs on a motorcycle rode down our street. One of them got off and asked Mami for her jewelry at gunpoint.

"Hand me all of it!" he commanded, pointing to

her gold necklace. Mami, worried about her inherited diamond ring, turned the stone toward her palm and hid it in her fist.

"Can you remove it yourself? I need a mirror to do it," she lied to distract the thug. Amazingly, he believed her and took the necklace off.

These robberies had become commonplace on the island, and Mami knew how to handle them. She kept her cool right up until the mugger heard the piano. That was me inside busy practicing my piece with only our terrier, Pinto, for company.

"Who's in there?" the mugger asked Mami, peeking in through the metal slats of the window. Mami became agitated. Pinto started to bark. The mugger must have thought he was too much trouble to deal with, 'cause he left.

Later, when I told Mami how the mugger had looked me up and down, Mami had a meltdown. By the end of the month, Papi had gotten a transfer to the Hyatt in Orlando and Mami had placed our house up for rent, setting in motion our move to the United States right before school started. Brígida seethed when she found out. *It's all your fault, Luci* were her last words to me for months.

I'm glad we moved to Kissimmee. Here at Beaumont Middle School I met Karen in front of my locker. It's right next to hers. She's also from Puerto Rico. Her family moved to the Orlando area when she was little, so her English is perfect and she knows everything about being an American. We liked each other right away. We live in the same neighborhood, get hungry for garlicky plantain *mofongo*, and love Shakira. We became best friends on the first day of school, and, since that moment, we like to do everything together.

One Saturday Karen found this new Shakira video on YouTube and ran to my house to tell me about it. She was so excited that I quit my piano practice to go watch it with her on the family computer. We turned the volume up and went crazy trying out our diva moves.

"*¡Ay, bendito*, Luci!" Karen exclaimed. "Loosen up, *nena!*"

"Like this?" I asked, twirling my hips as fast as I could.

We sang the lyrics at the top of our lungs, pealing with laughter until Brígida got up from the sofa and turned the computer off.

"I need to study, Luci. Besides, have you seen your dance moves in the mirror?" she said with a sneer.

I opened my mouth in an attempt to respond with something witty, but, as usual, I froze. Puzzled, Karen looked at me and then at Brígida's smirk.

A few days later, on the way to school, I told Karen the story I had always kept to myself—the story about Brígida's made-up song.

"Brígida is a bully," my friend declared in the tone of voice she had learned from her mother, a psychologist.

"Bully?" I asked as we were getting out of the bus. "What's that?"

"Tu hermana," Karen answered. "Your sister." And she disappeared down the hall, late for geometry class. I thought about this new word for a long time. English was a language I was still learning. Back in Puerto Rico, I had never heard the word.

On my way to second period I spotted a couple of flyers on the wall. They had been there all along, but this time the word *bully* caught my eye. One flyer pictured school lockers spray-painted with names and slurs; the other showed a big ugly male cartoon character shoving a smaller one. Brígida didn't write slurs or push me. She taught me to respect her because she was the oldest, the *firstborn*. Birth order seemed to be *really* important to her. It kind of allowed her special rights. She made sure I knew that.

I'd been about six years old the afternoon my mother caught me kneeling before Brígida, sliding her feet into her fuzzy baby-blue slippers.

"Luci, what are you doing?"

"My job," I said, looking up at my sister. "Right, Brígida? ¿*Verdad*?"

Brígida had told me it was my duty to remove her shoes as soon as we got home from school. She was the firstborn.

"Brígida! What's wrong with you? Don't ask your sister to do that again!"

Brígida was mad. As soon as Mami left the room, she took the fancy taffeta-and-sequin gown Abuela had sewn for my Barbie doll and put it on hers. She declared that my doll couldn't wear it again until she said so and threatened to never play Barbies with me if I told Mami. It seemed like forever before Brígida allowed my doll to wear the gown once more.

I don't know why I told Karen about the song Brígida made up about me in Tórtola. It used to be a secret, a thing I was ashamed of. But Karen started asking questions on the bus, and it made me feel better to tell her. I had just turned eleven when we went on vacation. We were staying in a one-room cottage, and we sisters had finished settling in the common area. Looking for privacy, I turned my back to my sisters and faced the flamingo-pink wall to change into my bathing suit. When Brígida realized I was uneasy, she began chanting: "She's hiding chickpeas, teeny-tiny chickpeas / but has no chickpeas, teeny-tiny chickpeas." Her tune was as contagious as her laughter, and soon four-year-old Ani joined in a jingle she didn't understand.

"Chickpea! Chickpea!" Ani shouted gleefully.

Brígida laughed and put Ani on her shoulders and spun her around and sang the catchy chant with her over and over again. I endured the chant day after day and grew so self-conscious that I started wearing a T-shirt over my bathing suit at all times. Finally, one afternoon I complained to Mami. Brígida was quick to say that I was way too sensitive for my own good, that it was only a joke. Mami believed her. I felt alone within my family and became an expert at hiding behind my piano whenever I was home, to avoid being Brígida's target.

The school day flew by, and after gym class I picked up my things and headed for the bus. Karen was waiting for me at our usual seats.

"Hey, how about going to the movies later?" she asked.

"*¡Sí!*" I said at first. And then I remembered. "Oh no! I can't. I have to babysit for Ani. My parents are taking Brígida to the employees' party at the Hyatt, where Papi works."

"You're not going?" asked Karen.

I pouted. "They couldn't find a sitter, so I offered to do it."

"Okay, let's do something tomorrow, then."

"*Seguro,*" I said. "Sure."

When I got home, Brígida opened the door.

"You're all sweaty," she said. "You smell." She walked back into the hallway and stood in front of the full-length mirror, Pinto next to her. "You like my new skirt? Mami says I look stunning," she bragged, checking her slender self from all angles. "Hmm, who knows the guys I'll meet, right, Pinto?"

Brígida scratched Pinto just the way he liked.

Mami came down the stairs. "Luci, the piano teacher called. She thinks you might be the closing number at the end-of-the-year recital," she announced as she picked up her purse. "Remember you're in charge of dinner for both you and Ani! We'll be back around ten."

"Too bad you can't go," Brígida whispered. "No chickpeas allowed." She laughed at her own joke and left.

I was upstairs getting out of the shower when my little sister knocked on the bathroom door.

"Luci! I'm hungry!" she called. "I want french fries. Please?"

"Later," I said as I slipped into my shorts and

tank top. "After I dry my hair."

"But I'm hungry now!" she wailed.

I wrapped the towel around my long, dripping hair and climbed down the stairs to the kitchen. I took out a bag of frozen fries and placed it on the counter. Then I poured half a bottle of corn oil into the large frying pan on the stove. I turned the burner onto medium heat and left to blow-dry my hair while the oil got hot. Just before entering the upstairs' bathroom I drew Ani's attention away from Pinto and her cartoons to tell her that I would make the fries when I finished drying my hair. I was whistling Shakira's "Waka Waka" song, with the dryer's noise echoing around the bathroom tile, when I heard something that sounded like Pinto barking. Ani popped her head in the door.

"Luci," she whined. "Pinto is going crazy." She coughed. "My eyes hurt. Is something burning?"

"The french fries!" I yelled.

I ran down to the kitchen. The room was pitch-dark. I flipped the light switch but it was already on. Out of the pan, flames rose into dark plumes of smoke that turned the kitchen ceiling completely black. At the top of the stairs Pinto barked frantically. Ani stood next to him, her eyes wide with fear.

"Take Pinto back to your room, close the door, and open the window!" I screamed, tying up my hair with the scrunchie on my wrist.

I grabbed the pan with my left hand and stood in the middle of the kitchen, away from any wood cabinets or furniture. The yellow-and-blue flames danced on the surface of the oil. I stared at them, thinking. *How do I put out a fire?* A frenzy of images flashed by, and I remembered a cartoon. Water. Douse it with water. I tightened my grip on the pan and reached over to the sink to turn on the faucet with my free hand. I filled a glass with water and poured it all at once onto the burning pan. Flames raged out. Bursts of oil scalded my hand and wrist, running up my arm and sizzling a wisp of hair just short of my ear. I did not drop the pan. I stood there petrified. Not knowing what else to do, I waited for the fire to die down. Breathing acrid smoke. Streaming tears. Choking.

My parents and sister returned home as soon as I called. Brígida was furious with me for ruining her night, but not as much as she was a few days later when she found out Mami would not allow me to help repaint the kitchen ceiling and walls because of my injured hand.

"You know," Brígida said, glowering at me from atop her stool, "I'm the firstborn and shouldn't have to do this." She spoke in a way that made me feel like I had done the whole thing on purpose.

I spent the next few weeks applying ointment and dressing the burn on my hand twice a day. It had developed a hundred pearl-like blisters too awful to look at. I cringed each time I applied the soothing cream the emergency-room doctor had ordered for the third-degree burn. At least at school Karen made me feel good. She always walked in front of me in the crowded hallways, opening a clear path to prevent other students from bumping into my hand.

By the middle of May the burn had finally healed. I was left with a wrinkled, raised white scar at the root of the mottled skin climbing up my arm. The good thing was that I could still play the piano, and I practiced my recital piece over and over. I had first learned it in Puerto Rico, and it brought back fond memories of evenings playing to a background chorus of *coquí* tree frogs.

For the end-of-the-year recital, I wore my lavender dress and glittery sandals. I was the last performer, and I walked onto the stage to a packed school auditorium. I smiled at Karen, who was sitting next to Brígida, Ani, and my parents in the front row. I played my piece without any mistakes. Applause filled the room with my final notes, and I stood to bow, feeling giddy with joy. At the reception that followed the recital, Karen spotted me and walked over, trailed by Brígida. Ani ran ahead of both of them and gave me a big hug.

"I'm going to get some cake now!" Ani announced.

"That was beautiful, Luci," Karen said, taking my left hand in hers. "You were so lucky that nothing really bad happened to your hand in that grease fire."

Brígida stood next to us, staring at me, at my hand, at Karen.

"At least you can play the piano, because no one will ever marry you with that scar. "¿*Verdad*, Karen?" Brígida grinned. Her icy-cold words felt like tiny daggers draining all the joy out of me.

I looked at her, desperately searching for the right comeback. I wanted to say something to make all the hurt go away. But instead it sank deeper and deeper into me. The pause grew longer, and I felt frozen in time, permanently speechless. Reading the feelings on my face, Brígida grinned wider.

"You're such a bully!" Karen snapped, showing the anger I couldn't.

All the color drained form Brígida's face, and she rushed to our parents, who were with Ani at the refreshments table.

"Luci's friend insulted me!" she screamed. Then she started retelling what had happened, making herself the victim.

"Calm, down, Brígida," Papi said. "Let's not blow things out of proportion."

"We don't want to make a scene," whispered Mami. "Let's go."

The drive back was a silent one. Karen's words rang in my mind. Was she right? I thought about our long talks on the school bus. I remembered the time that Karen's mother explained to me how a bully works: *If you take an isolated incident, it's not too bad, but bullies hurt you time and again over a long period through many of these seemingly insignificant incidents.* Yeah, there were scores of little things I had tried to erase from my memory, from the slippers to the chickpea jingle. I glanced at my hand and gently *touched* my scar.

I liked boys, but I wasn't planning to marry any-time soon. Would the scar go away by then? Would boys care? Did it even matter? *Bully*, a word that doesn't even exist in Spanish. I had looked it up. And if it's true, if Brígida is a bully, what do I do? She's still my sister. Mami always says that family comes first and you are loyal to your family no matter what. I suddenly felt the urge to play the piano to let the music blow away the whirlwind of my thoughts.

All summer I hung around with Karen, practiced piano, and played with Ani. Brígida was her usual self. She had this thing against me that I tried to ignore. I thought maybe one day she would change on her own. Or a time would come when I would have the courage to talk back, to make her see how hurtful she could be. What I didn't expect was that the change would come through Ani.

Ani was turning six, and she had asked for cake or ice cream cones to celebrate. So Mami and I came up with an idea of a three-tier yellow birthday cake with chocolate filling and frosting decorated with an empty sugar cone. We'd fill the cone with ice cream at the last minute. I knew Ani would love it. We spent the afternoon baking the cake while she played at the neighbor's house, and by the time she returned, it was finished and hidden away.

"Where's my cake?" Ani asked as soon as she came in the door, cheeks flushed pink.

"Es postre," Mami declared. "It's for dessert."

"I want to see it," Ani pleaded, cocking her head to one side.

"You'll have it soon enough," I told Ani. "Dinner is almost ready, right, Mami?"

Since Ani couldn't wait, we had dinner early. Brígida chatted with Papi. Mami and I busied ourselves frying *tostones*, serving seconds, and eating with relish. Right before dessert Karen stopped by and Mami invited her to stay. Brígida looked super annoyed.

"Today is my birthday, Karen!" Ani exclaimed, jumping out of her chair. "I'm six!"

"*¡Feliz cumpleaños!*" Karen congratulated Ani. She handed my little sister a birthday card. Ani opened it, and out came Karen's voice singing our birthday song: *"Feliz, feliz en tu día, amiguita que Dios te bendiga . . ."*

I ran to the piano and started playing the melody so all would join me in a second rendition of the song. Pinto wagged his tail wildly beside me. Mami rushed in with the birthday cake decorated with the filled ice cream cone, complete with sprinkles and a cherry on top, surrounded by six pink candles flickering brightly.

Ani's eyes sparkled at the sight of the cake. She brought her dimpled hands to her face and started clapping in total delight. The cake in front of her, her little fingers eager to dip into the frosting, her lips pursed to blow out the candles after making her secret wish: it was all beautiful to me. Mami gave the first piece to my little sister, adding the one and only ice cream cone on top, sprinkles, cherry, and all. Ani almost disappeared behind the tower of scrumptious sweets. Halfway through her cake she asked for milk.

"Brígida, *por favor*," Mami said. "Get her some milk."

Brígida left. When she returned, she placed a small glass of milk before Ani.

"Don't stuff yourself," Brígida told Ani. "You'll get even fatter."

"Why do you always call me fat?" Ani asked in a little voice.

In that instant Ani's question made everything clear. Something blurry came into sharp focus, and the arsenal of words that had been frozen within me began to thaw.

"Don't pick on Ani. She's beautiful," I said, looking at Brígida in the eye. "And she's our sister. You don't have the right to say mean things just because you're the firstborn. Mami? Papi?"

Karen looked at me and smiled with pride.

"Luci tiene razón," said Papi.

"I agree," said Mami. "Luci is right."

Brígida was stone-faced.

Ani sprung up and gave me a chocolatey kiss.

CUBANO TWO

Tal para cual

In a public middle school in Raleigh, North Carolina, the media specialist has left two kids alone in a windowless room. It's heating up to be a steamy summer day. Not that the kids can tell. The room is dimly lit except for a spot of light shining on a red sofa and a checkered rug. A few cameras mounted on tripods point to the sofa, where a tiny media player lies. Standing on different colored squares of the rug, the students—sometimes described as the Monster and the Rascal—don't

know they've both been chosen to be the new hosts of the morning news show. (Sorry, nothing sinister here.) They're eighth graders, boys, and *Cubanos*. Their ethnicity has nothing to do with their personalities. Or maybe it does. The Monster, who came into the studio first, speaks up.

"What are you doing here? You bony, Dumbo-eared newbie to my school who looks like a squirrel monkey looking for his mama."

> "Tell you what, you whale-like knuckle-dragging ape with a flabby belly spilling over shorts that want to be pants but are not. I'm the new news host. I'm the new, the new, the new news host. *Tum, pakatum, pakatum, pantum*."

"Say what? *I* am the new host. You just fresh-from-the-island kid singing *cumbia* instead of salsa? What do you know about my school in my America?"

"*Your* America? We *all* live in *América.* *Sudamérica, Norteamérica,* Cuba—*ay,* yes, Cuba's in *Norteamérica.* Cradle of the queen of *your* salsa. *¡Rica azúcaaa'!*"

"My *abuela* is Pedro Pan. She was sent away from Cuba to the land of the free and she's worked hard, really hard to be someone. And I was born here. What do you say to that, fresh-from-the-island kid?"

"Your *abuel-A* is Pedro Pan? No, no, no, your *abuela* is Pe-TRA Pan, Petra Pan for a layedeee: *pedropan-petrapan-pa-ca-tan-tan-tan.*"

"Abuela says that your Cuba was run by a thief. A thief who stole from his countrymen. We are exiles; you're just an immigrant."

"Exile, immigrant—just labels, *chiquitico.* Just labels. They kick you out, you leave. You're gone 'cause of politics, or you leave 'cause there's nothing to eat. Same old, same old. Now we're both in a great land. The land of the brave, the brave and free, to be the best, the best that we can be."

"Abuela says you newly arrived have no idea how to be the best at anything. You just know how to *resolver*, patch things up until the next crisis."

"*Oye, chiquitico,* lemme ask you somethin'. Can you think for yourself? 'Cause it sure sounds like you use your *abuela*'s brain to think and talk, if you know what I mean."

"Uhh . . ."

"And another thing. Why you suppose we're both here? Maybe we're *iguales*? Equally good to be the new, the new, the new news hosts. Aha! *Sí, sí.* The new, the new news hosts."

"Equally good?"

"Never occurred to you, huh? *Tum, pakatum, pakatum, pantum.*"

"Is that the Pichy Boys you're humming? Give me the player. Here! Hear—your—*cumbia.*"

"I knew you'd come around. We both have the *música* inside. Stand next to me, join the *vacilón!* Right foot front and right foot back and kick and sidestep and swirl them hips, and front and back and back and front and add *sazón, sazón, sazón.*"

"*Tum,* pakatum, pakatum, *pantum.*"
"Tum, *pakatum, pakatum,* pantum."

Ten minutes later the media specialist returns to find Rodolfo, the Monster, and Pablito, the Rascal, dancing side by side—each doing his own thing—to the music emanating from the earbuds they share. Now things are heating up indeed. You can feel the heat both outside and when you come back in. . . .

PEACEMAKER

Las aguas siempre vuelven a su cauce.

He could still hear them, even with earphones on
and behind the closed doors of his dark room. Wilfred could hear Mom and Papi at it, while he tried
to think of the next move in his chess video game.
Bright sunlight outlined the window's closed
blinds, and he felt the mood inside his home as
oppressive as the summer heat of New Orleans.
Yes, they were fighting again, like almost every
time they were together. He knew what he had to
do. And he was delaying it as long as he could.

But in the small silences between loud voices he could hear the faint sobbing of his younger sister, Blanca. For her, once more.

He remembered the first time he did it, two years ago. He had just turned eleven. He and Blanca had been playing a board game on the front veranda with Abuelo asleep at the far end, an empty beer bottle on his lap. Theirs was a house Wilfred's grandparents had bought a long time ago because Abu Celeste, his grandmother, said it reminded her of her native Nicaragua. When Abuelo could no longer pay its mortgage, Papi took it over even though he'd never liked the house. A pink house with tall arched windows that opened onto a veranda lined with white rocking chairs. Wilfred and Blanca were sitting under the window that had been left cracked open, when they heard Papi's screams. "It's always the same!" Papi thundered. "Too many opinions in this house! Too many people living in it! What do you want? Talk to me!" Each string of words boomed louder than the last one, until it seemed like the old window panes would shatter under the pressure of the sound waves.

Blanca's lower lip began to quiver, and she started to sob. Blanca made her five-year-old body tiny and crawled under one of the four rocking chairs. She pressed the sides of her head with her hands until the tips of her ears turned red and the back of her hands white. Wilfred tried coaxing Blanca out from under the chair with the promise of candy, of playing her favorite game, of pushing her on the swing, but she wouldn't budge. Because he didn't know what else to do, Wilfred knelt and kissed his sister on the head. And as Blanca lifted her gaze up to him, she whimpered, "Make them stop, Wilfred. Make them stop."

Wilfred held his breath. He rose and walked toward Abuelo to ask for help. Wilfred shook Abuelo until the bottle fell to the floor of the veranda and rolled out onto the lawn. Abuelo grunted from deep within his slumber and shooed

Wilfred away like a pesky fly. Wilfred saw that he had no choice. He adjusted his eyeglasses and walked inside. That was the first of many more times. And each time he would end up doing the same thing. Taking messages from Papi to Mom, from Mom to Papi. With each trip, Wilfred would change hurtful words for softer ones, until things quieted down and the calm he and Blanca craved returned for a bit.

Wilfred closed his laptop and went out into the hall. In the room across from his, he saw Abu Celeste holding on to her knotted wooden cane, praying in front of the Purísima's altar. Blanca sniffled by her side. Abuelo had carved Abu Celeste an intricate maple pedestal for the statue of Nicaragua's beloved Virgin Mary. It now sat atop their dresser, with the painted plaster statue surrounded by votives, silk flowers, and candy. Wilfred looked at the altar and wondered how many other beautiful things Abuelo would have created if he hadn't started drinking years ago.

Abu Celeste crossed herself and took the last piece of *gofio* from the altar to hand to Blanca. Blanca loved Abu Celeste's special corn-and-sugar candy, but she shook her head no.

Wilfred sighed. He climbed down the stairs and went into the kitchen to broker the peace once more.

By the end of the summer, the fights were much more frequent than the bits of calm in between. Most of the time Wilfred couldn't tell why the fights happened. But he knew that they were getting to be too much to bear, and he looked forward to the start of school. The year before, in seventh grade, he had joined the chess club. He liked it much more than group sports. Practice was held after school, with tournaments on Saturdays. This year, with the captain of the team now in high school, Wilfred thought he had a shot at being elected captain. But two weeks into the school year he learned that chess club had been canceled, even with ten kids signed up. The club's sponsor had fallen ill and no replacement had been found.

One September afternoon he arrived home to find Titi Claudia and Tío Gonzalo visiting. Titi Claudia was in the kitchen with Mom, who was off from work at the hospital. They were unloading groceries in a flurry of activity. Papi had not arrived yet.

"¡Hola, Wilfred!" Titi Claudia greeted Wilfred with a bear hug.

"Tell him, Claudia," Mom prompted as she started marinating some chicken.

"Want to hear the news?" Titi Claudia teased with hands on her hips.

"Yeah?"

"Your *titi* now has her own pastry shop!" Titi Claudia giggled, clapping furiously. "I'm taking over the famous French bakery on Ursulines Avenue. The owner is retiring. My dream! Right in the French Quarter!"

"Oh," Wilfred said.

"Wilfred!" Titi Claudia exclaimed, shaking Wilfred by both shoulders. "Aren't you excited? I'll be able to make croissants, French baguettes, little sweet cakes, all the things you like so much!"

Titi Claudia went on to say that the bakery was in really good shape. She was thinking of giving it a fresh coat of paint and maybe changing its name. Or maybe not.

"I'd love for you to come on Saturdays and Sundays to help. You could learn a thing or two at the shop!" she said to Wilfred.

As Titi Claudia talked, she paired each sentence with hand flourishes here and there, like she always did. Wilfred stared at her and thought about how much lighter the house felt when she was around.

"Go, go, change," coaxed Titi Claudia. "We're going to celebrate at dinner with a feast!" she added, arching her painted eyebrows.

Dinner was delicious. After clearing the table, they all gathered in the living room to see the pictures of the bakery. Titi Claudia had brought swatches of the paint she was considering for the shop's walls, and Blanca amused herself arranging them by hue. Tío Gonzalo shared projections of possible future earnings. Papi gave his younger brother advice on hiring and managing personnel. Abu Celeste talked recipes with Titi Claudia, who seemed to like the idea of expanding the French offerings to include some traditional pastries from Latin America.

"*¡Ay!* How about *buñuelos*?" Abu Celeste asked from her comfortable chair, her withered hands resting on top of her cane.

"*Sí, sí*, why not?" Titi Claudia said. "Syrupy fritters could be a big success!"

"*Pan dulce* and *gofio*," Abu Celeste added. "For the Purísima celebration and Christmas!"

"Abu Celeste's *gofio* is the best!" exclaimed Blanca, picking up all the paint swatches from the coffee table and throwing them high in the air.

"Oh, I'll make another batch this December,"

added Abu Celeste with a chuckle. "I promised the celebration committee at church that I would bring the candy again. It will be great to all go as a family!"

"Oh, no, no," interrupted Papi, lifting his head from Tío Gonzalo's documents. "Don't count on me for the Purísima. I hate having to be nice to people I don't care about."

"Wilfredo, *por favor*," pleaded Mom. "The whole family has to go."

"You, don't tell me what to do!" barked Papi.

"Wilfredo, this is important to Abu Celeste," Mom said in a measured voice. Wilfred noticed Abu Celeste tightening her grip on her cane.

"Well, I'm not saying she can't go," noted Papi as he rose from the sofa and went to the windows. "But I'm not going. And that's that!" He began to close all the shutters.

Abuelo went to serve himself a shot of rum, mumbling to himself.

"Mami," Mom told Abu Celeste, "come help me

in the kitchen, please."

Blanca walked over by Wilfred. Wilfred placed his long arm around his sister's small shoulders. Titi Claudia and Tío Gonzalo collected their things and quietly left.

By the end of November, Wilfred had helped at the bakery fourteen times. It felt good to be out of the house. Sometimes Tío Gonzalo gave him a ride; other times Wilfred would ride the bus into the French Quarter. He started by helping at the register but soon moved into the kitchen, where he had already learned how to make bread dough. Titi Claudia said he was a natural. Wilfred liked to mix all the bread ingredients and knead the soft dough. He liked knowing that as long as he followed all the steps, the bread would always turn out well. Sometimes during his break, Wilfred walked down Ursulines Avenue and across the train tracks to the banks of the Mississippi River. Then he would look at the level of the water and notice how it rose and receded depending on the weather. He'd heard stories of water filling everything years ago. The water damage could still be seen in buildings throughout the city. Staring at the river, he thought about his parents and worried about Blanca. Grown-ups had always told him that a good boy, *un hombrecito*, was gentle with girls and protected them. He wanted to be a good boy. Blanca had been born when he was six, and from the moment he'd first seen her, he'd wanted to protect her.

As December approached, the businesses around Titi Claudia's bakery began to hang thick garlands of greens and multicolored glass balls from the intricate ironwork of their balconies. Slender Christmas trees flanked the shops' entrances, and long strings of blinking lights outlined the colonial architecture of the French Quarter. Titi Claudia had added *pan dulce* to the season's offerings and taught Wilfred how to fold the nuts and candied fruit into the egg bread dough. Each time Wilfred worked his fists into the dough, he thought of Abu Celeste making *gofio* and . . . the tension building at home. It reminded him of Titi Claudia's words: *Milk left on the fire too long always boils over.* This year, December 7, the feast of la Purísima, fell on a Monday. Just a week away. Abu Celeste had gotten very involved with the organizers and could not stop talking about the festivities. Every time she talked about it in front of Papi, he grunted and changed the subject. Each passing day made Wilfred more anxious.

On Sunday December 6, the whole house smelled of toasted corn and spiced syrup. Blanca was seated at the kitchen table next to Abu Celeste. As Abu Celeste cut the *gofio* into diamond shapes, Blanca lined up the pieces one by one in perfect rows on the metal tray. Mom was washing dishes.

From his room Wilfred heard Papi come into the house early from work at the car dealership.

"Ah! It smells like Celeste's *gofio*," Papi

exclaimed. "Nicaragua's best!"

"*Gracias*, Wilfredo," said Abu Celeste.

"I think I need to taste it!" Papi announced, picking up one piece from the tray.

"Papi!" Blanca complained. "You're messing up my arrangement."

"Wilfredo, are you coming with us tomorrow?" asked Mom.

"I told you I'm not," said Papi. "Besides, I have a meeting."

"But tomorrow is your day off," replied Mom.

"Don't I have the right to have a meeting?" retorted Papi.

"Very well," Mom said, whisking the tray away and placing it on top of the refrigerator. "So nobody goes."

"*Ay, Elvira, por favor,*" protested Papi, "don't be so dramatic!"

Wilfred went to the landing and called Blanca to come up the stairs. He knew the storm was about to start. Blanca ran into Wilfred's room and hid under his bed. After the screaming and shouting ended, a stifling silence filled the house. That was usually the cue for Wilfred to get ready for his dreaded *duty*—to try to broker the peace, just like with every other fight. It was always Papi who gave in first. He could not stand Mom's silent treatment, and Wilfred would have to convey messages between them. Today Wilfred didn't want to. He just couldn't anymore. And he thought of something else.

"What are you writing?" asked Blanca, wiggling out from under Wilfred's bed.

"A note to Abu Celeste," said Wilfred. "Get your shoes. We're going."

"Where?" asked Blanca.

"I'll tell you later—hurry up. We need to leave now."

Wilfred could hear Mom in the laundry room, making herself busy. He knew Papi would be in his bedroom, staring blankly at the TV. Abu Celeste was probably trying to nap, with Abuelo passed out drunk by her side.

As soon as Blanca came back from her room with her shoes on, Wilfred told her to go wait outside. Then he peered into his grandparents' bedroom, made sure they were asleep, and slipped the note under the Purísima statue's pedestal. He gathered his backpack and tiptoed back down the hallway toward the stairs. At the top of the landing, Wilfred heard Papi call, "Wilfred!"

Wilfred froze. His stomach seized. Beads of cold sweat rose on his forehead. Should he answer his father? Just thinking of it made his feet feel like lead. Or should he leave? From the top of the stairs Wilfred made out Blanca's silhouette against the evening lights. She was bouncing from foot to foot on the veranda.

"Wilfred!" his father called again.

"I can't, Papi," Wilfred replied in a timid voice. "I can't!" he repeated, louder. "I won't!" he hollered. And before he could even think about what he'd done, Wilfred sprinted down the stairs and out of the house. "Follow me," he whispered to his sister. "We don't want to miss the bus."

They ran to the bus stop and caught the bus just in time. Wilfred had left his cell phone on purpose. He didn't want to be tracked. He had his money. The bus was halfway full, and Blanca chose a front window seat. The minute Wilfred sat next to her, she started asking questions.

"Where are we going?"

"To Titi Claudia's," answered Wilfred.

"Oh," said Blanca. "It's a short ride to her house, right?"

"No," answered Wilfred. "We're going to her bakery."

"All the way to the French Quarter?" asked Blanca, her eyes large in amazement.

"Uh-huh," answered Wilfred, already starting to have second thoughts. What if Titi Claudia had left early? He started tapping nervously with his left foot. To calm himself and distract Blanca he began to play a guessing game with her. They played it for a long while.

It was dark by the time they arrived to their bus stop. Wilfred held Blanca by the hand. He could feel her excitement as she pointed to each of the houses that were beautifully decorated with tiny Christmas lights. Nearing Titi Claudia's shop, Wilfred saw the *Closed* sign. He breathed deeply. He hoped Titi Claudia would be working in the kitchen, like she usually did. They walked through the alley and up to the back entrance. He rang the bell.

"Why are we here?" asked Blanca, looking up at her brother.

"Because maybe Titi Claudia can help us," answered Wilfred. Although he truly didn't know what kind of help he wanted. Or if Titi Claudia could even do anything. All he knew was that he couldn't handle the fights anymore. Each new fight chipped away a bit more of his eagerness to bring calm to the house, to keep the peace so Blanca could have a normal childhood. He was at a loss.

It wasn't like him, but he needed to talk.

"Okay," agreed Blanca as she stretched to push the doorbell again.

They waited in silence, listening for any movement in the bakery. From deep inside they heard Titi Claudia.

"Wilfred, Blanquita!" exclaimed Titi Claudia upon seeing them standing in the doorway. "What on earth are you doing here, and at this hour? Come inside!" she said, hugging each one of them tight. "What happened?"

Titi Claudia led them through the kitchen and to the nearest café table in front. As soon as Wilfred sat, he broke down. He wanted to say so many things about the tension and the fights and the pressure to be an *hombrecito* for Blanca, but all he could do was gasp and cry.

"Sorry," said Wilfred, wiping his nose with the back of his hand.

Blanca stopped munching the *pan dulce* Titi Claudia had given her and went to Wilfred. She kissed him on the cheek and placed her head on his shoulder. Titi Claudia took Wilfred's hand in hers. And little by little she gave words to his thoughts and feelings.

"So, was it your parents fighting?" Titi Claudia asked.

Wilfred nodded, hunched over.

"And you've reached your breaking point, ¿sí?"

"Mm-hm."

It was amazing how Titi Claudia could figure out his conflicting feelings. He was fed up with his role. He didn't want it anymore. Guilt overwhelmed him when he thought of it. Why couldn't he keep a lasting peace? Maybe he wasn't a good enough son. Maybe he wasn't worthy of being his sister's big brother. And now he was ashamed of talking back to his father.

"None of this is your fault, Wilfred," whispered Titi Claudia. "You're a wonderful son and an even better brother. Look at how Blanca loves you!" Titi Claudia threw her hands in the air.

141

Wilfred smiled at these words, looking at Blanca from the corners of his downcast eyes.

"It's like what happens to milk left too long on the fire, right?"

Wilfred pursed his lips and nodded in agreement. "Yeah," he said softly.

"You shouldn't have to bear the responsibility of keeping the peace between your parents," Titi Claudia continued. "Maybe Tío Gonzalo and I should talk to them. Truly, what you did today, to stand up to your dad, takes a lot of courage. In my book, it defines you as a man. *Todo un hombrecito.*" She looked at the clock on the wall. "Should we call your parents and let them know you're safe?"

"I left a note," offered Wilfred. "For Abu Celeste."

"Saying you came here?"

Wilfred adjusted his glasses and nodded yes.

"Will she see it?" asked Titi Claudia.

"Yep," said Wilfred. "At her prayers."

"She'll probably start praying as soon as they

find out you two are missing, right?" Titi Claudia said. Wilfred nodded again. Titi Claudia tapped her fingers on the table; she glanced at the clock and turned to Wilfred. She seemed ambivalent. Wilfred gazed into Titi Claudia's eyes, pleading his case. *"Bueno,"* she decided as she stood up. "If we don't hear from them in the next hour or so, we'll call."

The three of them went into the kitchen to get things ready for the next day. They were almost done with Titi Claudia's evening tasks when the store's doorbell rang. Wilfred's heart skipped a beat. Titi Claudia patted him gently on the back on her way to the bakery entrance.

Mom and Papi were standing outside the glass front door, the lanterns of Ursulines Avenue casting eerie shadows on their faces. As they came into the shop, Wilfred noticed Mom's glassy eyes and smeared mascara. Papi looked disheveled, older.

"Wilfred, Blanca, let's go home," Papi commanded in a hoarse and soft voice.

"Don't you want a *cafecito*?" asked Titi Claudia, walking to the espresso machine. "I can brew it in no time."

"Thank you, Claudia," said Mom. "It's late. Besides, my parents are waiting in the van."

"*¡Qué bueno!* The whole family came!" exclaimed Titi Claudia, trying to make light of it.

"Can I take *pan dulce* home?" Blanca asked Titi Claudia.

"Of course!" both Titi Claudia and Mom answered at once.

"Wilfred," Titi Claudia said in earnest as she held the front door open, "see you next Saturday, *¿sí?*"

"Okay," said Wilfred with a smile. He hugged her.

Wilfred took Blanca by the hand and followed Mom and Papi to the car. After walking half a block, Wilfred noticed how Papi slid his arm over Mom's shoulder. Blanca must have seen it too. She squeezed Wilfred's hand. It was a happy squeeze. He squeezed back. A hopeful squeeze.

As Papi started the van, all sat quietly inside.

Blanca broke the silence. "Are we going to la Purísima tomorrow?"

Wilfred looked at Blanca reproachfully. Blanca shrugged.

Papi pulled out of the parking space. Then he looked at Mom.

"Yes, we'll all go for a little while," he finally answered. Mom looked at Papi, then turned toward the window, leaning her head against the headrest.

At the bend in the corner Wilfred looked back. In the distance he could still make out Titi Claudia waving at them, waving at him.

Wilfred waved good-bye as they drove away into the deep purple New Orleans night.

THE SECRET

Mañana será otro día.

A ray of sun streamed through the window, spreading across the bedroom floor. Carla followed this light with her eyes to the collage-covered shoe box peeking out from beneath Esperanza's bed on the other side of the room. She knew her sister's new diary was inside, and she was curious. In the living room the TV was on, and Esperanza was probably watching. So Carla got up from her bed and gingerly closed the bedroom door. She retrieved the diary and read the last entry.

I used to love my name. Es-pe-ran-za. Soft
syllables that melt into one another like
spoonfuls of vanilla ice cream on a hot
Chicago afternoon. Now I cringe at the sound
of it when my mother calls, or my little sister
looks for me, or even at school when the
teacher hands out graded homework. I've been
hating my name since the day my mother told
me the truth about myself. The day I stopped
being an American. Esperanza means hope.
And I don't have any. I went from feeling like
the world was mine in the afternoon, to being
illegal by the evening. How can a person be
illegal? I haven't done anything wrong. My
little sister and brother were born here. They're
all citizens. They have all the rights. They
don't know I'm not like them. None of my
friends know, not even my best friend, Cindy.

Memories of that afternoon came rushing back
to Carla. Esperanza had returned from some

audition, so excited because she had been told she would be hired to dance in a music video. She just needed to provide her Social Security number. She pranced around the house, bragging to Carla about how *this* was her big break. She would have a real job and get paid for doing the thing that she loved most. And she would be dancing with super-cute guys. Her friend Cindy had agreed with Esperanza that she was the best of the girls auditioning that day. They were in the kitchen when Mami came home from work and Esperanza blurted out the news. Mami collapsed on a chair and rubbed her forehead as if trying to get rid of a headache. Then she ordered Carla to her room. Carla stepped out of the kitchen and hid in the hallway so she could overhear her mother's story.

"Esperanza, sit. *Te tengo que contar algo,*" Mami said. "I have to tell you something. I was your age when I gave birth to you in Oaxaca, México," she began as she leaned on the table. "Life down there, it was rough. No work. *Nada de trabajo, nada*. Tía Elsy had found work up here, and she convinced your dad and me to come join her. Papi, your abuelo, hired a *coyote* who crossed us over the Rio Grande on a moonless night. Papi later told me this man was the best smuggler he could afford. A Mexican American family drove you across the next day. They passed you off as one of their six children. From the moment I placed you in that woman's arms, I couldn't stop crying. Not even your dad could console me. I didn't know if I would ever see you again. But the *coyote* insisted that if you screamed, we would all get caught. So I gave in. You were only eight months old. There. Now you know the truth."

As soon as Mami finished speaking, an eerie silence fell over the kitchen. Carla remembers slipping into her room. She remembers the front door being slammed, and waking up at dawn to her sister's muffled sobs. For months now neither Esperanza nor Mami had brought up the subject again. Carla looked down at Esperanza's diary and kept on reading:

I think everyone born in the United States
is so lucky. At school, we recite the Pledge of
Allegiance every morning. I'm the one who
does it every day and doesn't sit right down. I
say it right. I want to be here. I want to learn.
I love this country more than my classmates
who were born here. I want to go to college. I
want to be a dance teacher. But I can't do that
unless I'm a legal citizen. I lose hope a lot.

Suddenly Carla heard Esperanza's footsteps
and snapped her sister's diary shut. She hid it
in the same box she had found it in. She bit her
plump lower lip and retreated to her bed, frown-
ing behind the library book she had been reading.

"What were you doing?" asked Esperanza, pushing the door wide open. "I saw you going through
my things."

"*Nada*," said Carla, looking over her thick eyeglasses.

"*¡Mentirosa!*" Esperanza fumed. "Liar!"

"I was just looking for my hair barrette," said

Carla, pulling down the T-shirt that kept riding up her belly.

Back when Carla was five and Esperanza was eight, Esperanza was her best friend. They played together all the time. But when Esperanza turned eleven, she stopped playing with Carla. The more Carla begged and nagged, the less Esperanza wanted to play. So one day Carla stopped asking and turned to books. Books became her best friends. Now, at eleven herself, she read all the time. She read school library books and public library books; she read the backs of cereal boxes and the junk mail that the postman delivered. Sometimes she would stop on her way home from school to read flyers posted on store windows.

Carla waited hopefully while Esperanza changed into her favorite shorts.

"I'm going to Cindy's," Esperanza said. "We're practicing a new routine for dance club." She took the collage-covered shoe box and placed it on the closet's top shelf with an airy gesture. Esperanza had a floaty way of moving through space. It made her look as if she was always searching for a new dance move.

"Can I go with you?" Carla asked. She loved watching her sister dance.

"*No!*" retorted Esperanza, grabbing her purse and walking out of their room.

Once Esperanza left, Carla looked up at the top shelf. She thought of what she knew about her sister now. Maybe Esperanza was so nasty with her because she was hurting. She started wondering: *What does it really mean to be illegal?* She needed to find out. So Carla texted her mother that she was going to the public library and left the house.

At the Lozano library she checked out a bunch of books and began reading. Then she went onto the computer and searched. She learned that her sister would not be able to work or drive. She lacked the documents—papers that said she had rights. Worse, she could be deported if she was found out.

She could be sent back to a country she'd never known.

As long as Carla could remember, she had wanted to be just like her sister: pretty, graceful, and popular. Esperanza seemed to make friends without any effort. Not Carla. There were kids at school who made fun of her, of how she dressed, of how she ate, of her eagerness to answer teachers' questions. When Carla and Esperanza had attended the same school, Esperanza had come to her rescue more than once. Even if they didn't spend time together anymore, Esperanza was there for her. Now that Esperanza was in high school, they had grown apart. Every time Carla walked by Dulcería Lupitas, she remembered how sometimes after school her sister would take her there to buy a *paleta de tamarindo*. Esperanza had a way of asking the shopkeeper that always resulted in them getting two tamarind lollipops for the price of one. But things had changed. Maybe now Esperanza wanted to be like her as much as she wanted to be like Esperanza.

On her way out of the library Carla glanced at the Pilsen community bulletin board. A flyer caught her eye. *Dream Relief Day*, it read, announcing a gathering in August. At this meeting people could apply to stay in America. Carla suddenly remembered that, way before she knew about her sister's status, she had read something about the president signing an order that would allow young law-abiding Latinos to stay and work in the United States as long as they were in school. This could be Esperanza's chance to be legal, just like Carla. Carla stretched up on her toes to reach and tear the top flyer from the stack pinned to the board. She went to the listed website and read all about it. Carla needed to tell her sister about this opportunity, but how? She would have to admit that she had listened to their mother's story. Maybe even say that she had read her sister's diary. What if Esperanza got mad? What if she got so upset that she would never ever talk to Carla again?

When Carla arrived home, Esperanza and Cindy were leaning against the white iron railing by the front steps of the brick building.

"I don't understand you," Cindy said. "Why aren't you applying? You're the perfect dancer for this job."

"It's not for me," said Esperanza.

"You're wrong," said Cindy. "This is a big deal. Just like last fall. The video job? You never went back. Why?" Cindy saw Carla approaching and waved hello.

"I gotta go," said Esperanza, going up the steps to the front door.

"Yeah, me too," said Cindy, walking away. "My shift starts in half an hour. *I* have a job."

Sighing, Esperanza climbed the remaining steps.

Carla came up behind her sister and pulled her by the shirt. Biting her lower lip, she unfolded the flyer she had taken off the bulletin board and placed it into Esperanza's hands. In the end she would rather have a sister who was mad at her than a sister living hundreds of miles away in another country. Esperanza read the flyer and looked at Carla. She slid against the door and sank down to the floor, burying her face in her hands. She started to cry.

"I'm tired of making up excuses about why I'm not applying for jobs," Esperanza wailed. "I wish I didn't have to hide or lie and say that I was born in some random place," she said, sobbing.

Carla took out a tissue from her jeans pocket and handed it to Esperanza.

"What am I going to do?" Esperanza asked, tears smearing her mascara.

Carla sat next to her sister. "They say that if you're in school and have been here for at least five years you can apply for a permit to work," offered Carla.

"How do you know all this?" asked Esperanza.

"I read it on their website," said Carla.

"And you also read my diary," said Esperanza. "I should be mad at you."

"I know," said Carla. "I'm sorry."

Esperanza sniffled and smiled a little smile. "So, what do I need to apply?" she asked.

"Well, that's the thing," said Carla. "The application fee is four hundred sixty-five dollars."

"What?" Esperanza dropped her head back, shaking it in disbelief.

That evening Carla and Esperanza made a list of all the possible ways to raise money. They could ask Mami, but Esperanza didn't want to. She wanted to raise the money herself. Besides, ever since Papi left them, Mami had worked two jobs and was always complaining about how hard it was to pay the bills. They could have a bake sale, but neither of them knew how to bake. Maybe they could wash cars. Esperanza had once seen a movie where teens did that. But where would they do this in the middle of the city? They would need the water, soap, supplies. It seemed complicated. Then Carla thought that they could ask the librarian at the Lozano library for a job. Esperanza pointed out that it was unlikely they would get one, since Carla was too young and Esperanza had no Social Security number. They needed a job where no Social Security number was required.

"This might not work," Esperanza finally muttered, running her fingers through her highlighted hair. "Ugh, my hair is a mess. I need to go to Tía Elsy's for a haircut," she said.

"Tía Elsy!" Carla and Esperanza exclaimed in unison.

They couldn't believe that they hadn't thought of the beauty salon before. Esperanza told Carla that the best part of this plan was that Tía Elsy already knew she was illegal, although they had never spoken about it. Yes, asking Tía Elsy for a job was a good plan. The sisters agreed not to tell Mami about it. They would go visit their aunt at her salon the following morning.

For the next seven weeks Carla and Esperanza went to Elsy's *Salón de Belleza* every afternoon. Esperanza swept the floors between clients, and on busy days Tía Elsy had her wash hair. That was the best part, because most clients liked Esperanza and gave her good tips. From the beginning Carla helped organize the products and magazines and would also fix coffee or tea for the women. But one day Carla grabbed an old issue of *Selecciones* and started reading aloud a story while a client was waiting for the color to process. The older women at the salon loved how Carla read, and from then on they requested that Carla entertain them as they had their hair or nails done. Each time they returned home, Esperanza hid all her wages and any tips inside her collage-covered box. Carla added her own tips. In time Carla saw the money in the box grow. And she realized that Esperanza was growing closer to her again.

A week before Dream Relief Day, Esperanza counted all the money. She had $325.

"It's not enough," stated Esperanza. "And we won't be able to make up the difference by Dream Relief Day."

"Let's ask Mami to pitch in," said Carla.

Mami was home talking with Abuelo, who had recently moved in with them and was settling in their little brother's bedroom down the hall.

"I told you I don't want to ask!" Esperanza shouted.

"*¿Qué pasa?*" Mami came into the room. "What is going on?"

"Esperanza needs money for the application to become legal," Carla spilled out.

"What?" Mami asked. She listened to the whole story before sitting next to Esperanza. She stroked Esperanza's hair, and Esperanza leaned on Mami's shoulder.

Abuelo had been standing in the doorway and stepped into the room.

"We could pawn some jewelry," he suggested.

"That's a great idea!" Mami said.

✳ ✳ ✳

On August 15 Carla and Esperanza woke up at four a.m., each having barely slept. The night before, they had compiled everything for the application: the report cards from ten years in US public schools, the Mexican birth certificate, Esperanza's current high school ID card, and the $465 processing fee. Carla had helped Esperanza with twenty dollars of her own savings. Mami and Abuelo had added the difference from the pawned jewelry.

Esperanza slipped into her worn backpack the sandwiches their mother had made for them before going to work. Carla brought along the novel she was reading. The sisters ran out the door to catch the train on the Pink Line. They changed to the 29 bus and walked the rest of the way to the Navy Pier. By the time they arrived, a sea of young people were already in line. There were kids listening to music, twentysomethings on the phone, and even young mothers with babies in tow. Behind the sisters the line quickly lengthened into the distance.

Carla saw Esperanza raise her gaze as if searching for something above her. A bright orange sun appeared against a pewter-and-lavender sky, painting the water below in soft hues. The Ferris wheel stood still on the pier's skyline.

The excitement of many thousands of young people around them was amazing. Carla and Esperanza could almost touch the energy.

"I had no idea we were so many," Esperanza mused. She walked a few steps as the line began to move and suddenly turned around to embrace Carla.

"How about if when we get back home we go to Lupitas for *paletas*? My treat."

"*Ay, ¡sí!*" exclaimed Carla with a little jump. "*¡Tamarindo!*"

Esperanza slipped Carla's right hand into hers and twirled a little dance around her, bumping into a young man in front of them.

"Sorry," she said with a giggle. "I'm Esperanza."

Turning to Carla, she repeated, *"Es-pe-ran-za."*

"Yep," said Carla, seeing in her sister's eyes the joy of a new beginning.

Hope.

PICKUP SOCCER

El fútbol es la única religión que no tiene ateos.

And here I go running circles around my big
  cousin Hector
down Valencia Street . . . *first loop* . . .
   techie dudes and start-up nerds going to
    play a game of *fútbol*
at the Mission Playground . . . *second loop* . . .
    been practicing to be the game's
    commentator
    for one, two, three weeks . . . *third loop* . . .
    becoming the Andrés Cantor of
     this century,

recording on my phone . . . *fourth loop* . . .
   can't wait to call play-by-play at the reserved
      brand-new turf
   on the old neighborhood field . . . *fifth loop* . . .
going by the hood's newest hipster coffee shop,
   I see a bearded guy
in a techie shirt greets nerdy cousin Hector . . .
sixth loop . . .
   Hector's gotten the permit through a cool City
      of San Francisco app
   he found out about at his new start-up job . . .
   seventh loop . . .
      the bearded guy climbs onto his shiny bike
         and passes us
      on his way to the field—
      OOPS! I bump into Hector . . .

"Hey! Stop running circles around me, Hugo!
Walk normal, will ya?"

Okay, okay, I get excited sometimes . . .
   calm down and scuttle by Hector's side to cross

Eighteenth Street
looking up and down pricey condos that popped
up where I used to live . . .
fumbling with the phone in my pocket,
I turn to scamper backward
and grin at Hector . . . he rolls his eyes and
shakes his head . . . I make him smile . . .
and me eyeing the black-and-white ball in his
hands,
make a sharp turn onto Cunningham Place
ahead of Hector . . .
Hector turns the corner and I grab the soccer
ball from him
to dribble it just one last short block to the
field . . .
past the painted mural on the brick wall and
a skinny guy smoking by the bar's open
back door and a grandma watering potted
plants on the sidewalk across the alley that
faces her pretty green house . . .
I waver, with the ball under my foot,
at the black iron gate

of Mission Playground, framed by a big
   pink bougainvillea . . .
   I raise my gaze to see the dudes and nerds
      dressed in crisp T-shirts
   towering over my neighborhood friends in
      the middle of the field . . .
Javi, Frankie, Beto, Marco, Willie, Pepe,
   Edwin, Martin, Chad, and Max,
here for a pickup game, all look puzzled . . .
me kind of puzzled too, look away and keep
   tight-lipped . . .
and the bearded techie guy says that the bunch
   of kids don't want to leave the field,
claiming they've arrived first to play seven-on-
   seven *fútbol* . . .
   I dribble the ball around Hector one more
      circle . . .
         watching, listening, feeling nervous . . .
         Hector, who now looks pissed off . . .
      Hector, who has planned this soccer game
         for weeks . . .

Hector proud of his new getting-out of-the-hood
     job, his going-places job, his
I-worked-my-ass-off-for-this job, his I-finally-
     belong job . . .
     Hector, who's turning red and green and
          shades in between . . .
          Hector, who searches deep in his backpack
               and pulls out the crumpled permit
               to brandish in front of my neighborhood
               friends . . .

"Hey!" Hector growls. "We've got first dibs!
Can't you r-e-e-e-a-d?"

Whoa, Hector! But dudes and nerds agree and
     curse and gesture and grimace and swear
and tower even higher over Javi, Frankie, Beto,
     Marco, Willie, Pepe, Edwin, Martin, Chad, and
Max . . .
     Max says the field has always been free . . .
          Chad adds no reservations

were ever required . . .

Martin asks what's this permit app they
talk about . . .

Edwin asks who's this app and what's the
fee? . . .

Pepe says he came to play because
he couldn't stand being stuck
in his tiny apartment
with five other people . . .

Willie dribbles his old soccer ball, practicing
Ronaldo's scissors move over and over again . . .

Marco lies on his back staring at the sky . . .

Beto ties his shoe, not wanting to get
involved . . .

Frankie leaves to look for his dad . . .

Javi glares at me and asks . . .

"Are you with these dudes?"

Frankie's heard this question and turns back
around, zooming in on me . . . now I have

thirty sets of eyes staring at me all at once . . .
puzzled eyes and furious eyes and hurt eyes
and tired eyes and can't-believe-you eyes and
you-better-do-something-about-it eyes and
you're-a-traitor eyes and who's-this-kid eyes
and you're-a-poor-idiot eyes and who-gives-a-
damn eyes and let's-just-play eyes . . . and I
stand at the edge of the field paralyzed and
look at the thirty sets of eyes one by one and
see without seeing and hear without hearing
and feel bathed in so many icy glares that I
kick the ball into the center of the group wanting to still do the play-by-play, to still be the
Andrés Cantor of this century, but most of all
wanting to . . .

I pull my phone out, turn it to record mode, fill
my lungs to the bursting point, and yell out:
"LIVE FROM MISSION SOCCER FIELD,
FOR THE VERY FIRST TIME . . . HOOD'S
ALL STARS AGAINST START-UP

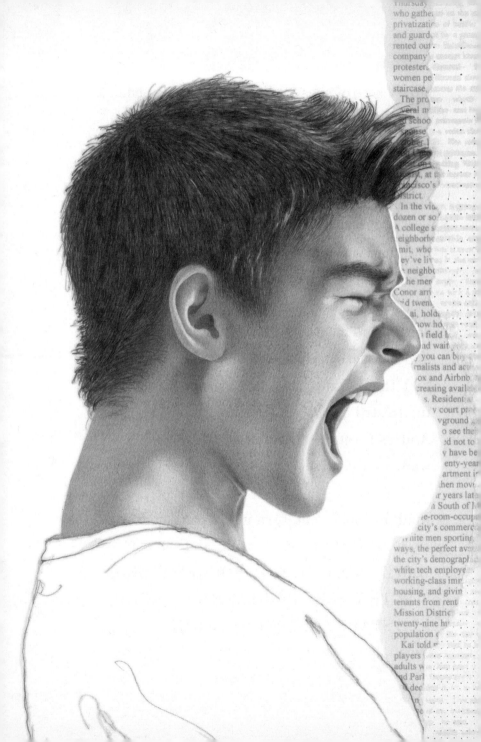

TECHSTERS . . . C'mon, players . . . give me a
*¡GOOOOOOOOOOOOOOOOOOOOOOOOOOOO
OOOOOOOOOOOOOOOOOOOOOLLLLL!!!"*

Silence.

Then one techie dude laughs out loud.
   Soon laughter ripples throughout the whole
      soccer field.
      A nerd says let's all play together.
         The neighborhood kids scream YES!
         ¡Órale! Finally!
      The players rearrange themselves.
   Hector looks at me kinda proud and—

The game's on!

SATURDAY SCHOOL

*Ser valiente es tener miedo a quedarse
sin hacer nada.*

I hate disappointing my parents. Education is important in my family. Three of my grandparents are university professors, and my parents are a doctor and a writer. So the other day when Mamá declared, *You need to learn correct Spanish, Sandra,* I did what I always do—keep quiet. And now, even though I'd rather not go to Saturday school, I'm on my way to Escuela Argentina on this chilly January morning.

Last Monday I heard Mamá talking on the

phone with Abuela. "Speaking and writing are two different things," Mamá told Abuela. "Sandra needs to read good literature and learn Spanish grammar." Abuela agreed and loudly ticked off the benefits of learning correct Spanish one by one: it would enrich my education; it would make me marketable; it could even find me the right husband. Really, a husband? I'm only eleven! But the worst was when Abuela said that it would make me stand out in public school. I feel already singled out! Not because I'm a straight-A student and won first prize at the science fair, but because I'm the only kid in the neighborhood elementary school whose parents speak Spanish at home. I was born in the United States and my parents are from Puerto Rico. And although I speak Spanish with them, I'm much more comfortable speaking English. It's the language of my friends. I want to fit in with them, but I want to please my parents, too.

After an hour in the car, Mamá takes the ramp

off the Beltway onto a street lined with tall oaks and maples and manicured lawns, and slows down before a huge lot with a double fence. I look twice. Two fences on the same lot? I've never been to this part of the county before. I see a white wooden rail fence by the curb, and a tall barbed-wire one twenty feet in. It's almost like the people in there don't know whether to welcome you or shoo you away. I start biting my cuticles.

"*¿Te pasa algo?*" Mamá asked. "Are you okay?"

"I'm fine," I lie. I stare at a few castle-like houses set far apart from one another. Who are the kids who live in them? Are they friendly? I look down at my new red tennis shoes to make sure their laces are neatly tied.

Mamá pulls into the driveway of a glitzy private school, explaining that the Saturday school is held here. The main office is identified by a flag, sky blue and white, trimmed in golden tassels. Once we're inside, Mamá introduces herself to the secretary. The lanky woman immediately starts talking in that form of Spanish that Abuela and Mamá use. It's not the Spanish I speak at home, the one I read in the children's books my grandma from Puerto Rico sends. This is the other Spanish. I always thought it was a code language between Mamá and Abuela. I feel a knot in my stomach. Is this the form of Spanish I'm supposed to learn? I can hardly understand Abuela! Mamá turns to me after handing the signed paperwork to the secretary. Her eyes sparkle the way they do when she's particularly happy or proud about something.

"*¡Vas a aprender mucho aquí!*" she says. "You'll learn a lot. I can't wait to hear all about it when I come back at two." She picks up her purse, ready to leave.

I can feel the knot in my stomach tighten. I glance at the clock on the wall. It's nine a.m. I want to tell Mamá that I don't want to stay. I have a bad feeling about all this. Hmm, maybe I could go back home and do all the chores I've been putting off? Just this once, I'm going to stand up for myself. I take a big breath that makes me feel strong and sure and ready just like a knight in shining armor.

Mamá speaks first. "I'm proud of you," she says.

And her words make my invisible armor crumble all the way to the floor. I fake a smile, say good-bye, and follow Mamá with my eyes as she walks away to her car.

Now I'm trailing the skinny secretary down a long hallway and up some stairs to the second floor. At the top of the stairs, she points to the corner classroom, room 25, and leaves. Am I supposed to go in by myself? From where I stand I can hear rowdy kids inside that room. I place one foot in front of the other, making the walk last longer than it should, until I reach my classroom and peer inside. There's a large poster board with a map of the Americas dotted with the places of origin of my classmates.

It seems like most of them are from Argentina. Do they all talk like the secretary and Abuela? I hope not. The kids are so loud that I can barely make out what they are saying. Here boys are trading soccer cards. Here girls are poring over pictures of a birthday party they all seem to have attended. It's like these kids have known each other for years and years. I feel a little sick. I want to call Mamá, but I remember the excitement in her eyes right before she left. *I can do this,* I say to myself. I spot a tanned girl with straight amber hair pulled back by a wide plaid hairband and approach her.

"*¿Tú sabes dónde me siento?*" I ask, looking around for a seat.

The girl looks at me, puzzled, "*¿Y vos, cómo te llamás?*"

I pause, trying to understand her question. My throat gets dry. I can feel both the girls and her friends staring at me.

"*Me llamo Sandra,*" I say. The group of girls

start to giggle. I take a step back and lean against the wall, wanting to fade into it. I listen with all my senses, trying to understand what I've said or done wrong. All I've said is my name! And then I know why the girls laughed. It's because of *how* I pronounce the words in Spanish. Loud steps announce the teacher at the door.

"*Buenos días, chicos,*" the teacher greets the class.

"*Buenos días, Señora Peña,*" the students answer in unison. Señora Peña looks like she's been out sunbathing for many years. Her large gold earrings dangle from her wrinkled earlobes. She looks my way and I straighten.

"*Ché, Mauricio, encontrále un pupitre a la chica nueva, ¿querés?*" Señora Peña asks a boy while gesturing toward me. I figure the teacher is asking him to find me a seat. *Encontrále, querés . . .* I repeat these words to myself.

"*¿Sos Sandra, no?*" Señora Peña asks. *Encontrále, querés, sos . . .* what is it about these words?

They are verbs! It dawns on me what the teacher and kids are doing that is different. They are conjugating the verbs all *wrong*. It's not the way Mamá taught me, back when I first learned to read. I was four then, and I remember that the Spanish textbook was written in the Spanish we spoke at home. Could it be that I've learned incorrect Spanish all along?

Seated at the corner desk in the last row, I pay close attention in class. I want to do well. I'm used to it. The teacher distributes copies of a story. She asks us to read it silence. At least the story is in the Spanish familiar to me and I understand everything. Then Señora Peña calls on the students to read aloud. One by one, the kids read the sentences in that peculiar singsong way Abuela has. They pronounce the words they read a different way than me or most of the people I've heard speaking Spanish do. When it's my turn, I rise and try to mimic my classmates' pronunciation. But this slows my reading. I can tell that Señora

Peña is losing patience.

"Gracias, Sandra," Señora Peña says. "Thank you. Maybe you can practice reading at home."

Some kids start to giggle. I've never felt this dumb. I feel my ears turning red.

"¡Mirá sus orejas!" I hear a boy yell. "Look at her ears!"

"Mauricio!" the teacher reprimands the boy.

I pull my hair over my ears, wanting to disappear under my desk. The teacher begins to ask questions about the story. I know all the answers but I'm terrified to raise my hand. I don't want to be mocked for how I speak! So I spend the rest of the morning in silence, wishing for time to pass.

The lunch bell finally rings, and all the students storm out the door.

"Sandra, vení, a almorzar," Señora Peña calls me to follow her to lunch. But then another teacher comes searching for Señora Peña and I'm left stranded by myself. I stand still for a moment, not knowing what to do. Then I venture into the

hall. My stomach is growling. I'm so hungry! I look one way, then the other. I've no idea where the cafeteria is, and I'm afraid to ask anyone for directions. I walk to the end of the hall, trying to follow the trail of voices, but I find myself at a dead end. Then I go down the stairs, passing by the main office, but the cafeteria doesn't seem to be there either. The cavernous building begins to feel more and more like a maze. I cry. Angry tears burn my cheeks in the middle of the empty hallway while I walk aimlessly. By the time the smell of pizza and hot dogs finally leads me to the cafeteria, lunch is already over.

That afternoon I wait to be picked up. I feel utterly alone. The minute Mamá pulls up, I run to the car. I have never felt this thrilled to see Mamá.

"It looks like someone had a good day!" Mamá says. "*Cuéntame,* tell me all about it. You liked it, right?"

I look into Mamá's eyes and see the usual

sparkle of pride. So I give in, again, wanting to please.

"Yes," I say.

"*¡Cuéntame, cuéntame!*" Mamá pleads, wanting to hear the details of my day.

"Well . . . ," I start. I wish there was something I could do to get out of attending Saturday school. And as we drive past the lot with the two fences, it occurs to me that someone might see the white fence and never notice the barbed-wire one. We stop at the red light.

"*Vos, no sabés lo que aprendí yo,*" I say, mimicking the singsong way of speaking they have at Saturday school and conjugating the verb Abuela's way.

Mamá turns to me.

"Why are you speaking as if you were from Argentina?" asks Mamá.

And I think again of the two fences and that maybe there are times when you need to point out the hidden one to others. I will have the courage this time. I don't want to return.

"That is how they teach Spanish, Mamá," I say. Then I tell Mamá how the kids made fun of the way I speak and how I was afraid to raise my hand. I tell her how I wish there was another way to learn correct Spanish. Mamá says nothing. But I notice she's upset.

I start picking my cuticles. I hope Mamá is not too angry with me. We're entering our neighborhood when Mamá speaks again.

"I had no idea they would all be speaking Argentinean Spanish. I should have inquired about this. It's my fault. No wonder you felt out of place. I want you to learn the Spanish most people use. The Spanish I learned in school in Puerto Rico, the written Spanish widely used by Spanish-speaking countries. We'll find another way."

"We will?" I ask, amazed that I stood up for myself *and* didn't anger Mamá.

"We could read together," Mamá says.

"We could . . . start our own Spanish book club?" I say.

Mamá pulls into the driveway, shifts the car into park, and turns to look at me. She has that sparkle in her eyes.

And I think my eyes . . . are sparkling too.

90,000 CHILDREN

Sólo el que carga el costal sabe
lo que lleva adentro.

Frank prepared his slingshot. He brought it to a full draw before raising his arms and aiming at the target. He leaned his cheekbone against his knuckle, the way Dad had taught him. Since school had let out for the summer in Mission, Texas, Frank had spent his days honing his shooting skills in his backyard. There was a shooting range nearby, and Dad had told Frank that now that he was twelve, he would teach him how to shoot a pistol. Once Frank knew how, they would go hunting with Gramps at his ranch in Duval County. Frank couldn't wait to learn how to shoot a gun.

Frank released the ammo with a light touch and hit the soda can hanging in the catch box that he and Dad had built. Fifteenth perfect shot in a row. He was getting really good. If he could go with Dad on his rounds, Frank knew he could shoot those illegal aliens in the ankles and make them swim all the way back to Mexico! Frank gathered his things and put them away. He didn't want Mom complaining. Mom frowned on Frank shooting and such. She much preferred it when Frank passed his time drawing superheroes. He liked doing that, too. Frank picked up his how-to manual to improve the hero's action pose that he had started the day before. Mom and Dad would be home soon. Frank was itching to hear Dad's latest story about his Border Patrol job.

Just a few months ago, Dad had been on night

patrol when he spotted footprints near the riverbank of the Rio Grande. He followed the trail stealthily to find seven men sleeping in the brush. Dad could tell they had crossed the border illegally. As he tied up one of the men, the others rose to flee, but Dad was quick to call in reinforcements. Less than an hour later every one of those illegal aliens was in handcuffs. Dad had told Frank that as soon as he noticed the backpack stress marks on the one guy's shoulders, he knew they had smuggled drugs. That's how these *mojados* paid the Mexican drug cartel for passage. Dad and the other agents searched for drugs and recovered seven fifty-pound bundles of marijuana hidden in the bushes.

Frank wanted to be just like Dad when he grew up. He wanted to get rid of the bad guys. Yeah, Frank would go to college so he could also enter into the force as a GL-11. College and experience had allowed Dad to climb quickly through the ranks at the Rio Grande Valley Sector. Dad was a boss. He spent a lot of time behind a desk, but he also spent a lot of time in the field, where the stories Frank lived for happened.

Frank heard Dad's truck pull into the driveway and rose to open the front door.

"Hey, Dad!"

Dad removed his bulletproof vest and handed it to Frank. "Hang that up for me, will ya, Frank? Be there in a minute."

Frank carried the heavy vest into Dad's study. He was about to hang it up when instead he tried it on. He looked at his reflection in the window. He looked good with his high brow and chiseled features. Gramps had said that he sure had Spanish blood running through his veins. He was *un verdadero* Francisco. A true Francisco, like his Tejano namesake, six generations ago, who had settled in what back then was New Spain. Baptized Francisco by his mother, nicknamed Frank by Dad. He loved his nickname.

Frank heard the front door opening and

removed the heavy bulletproof vest.

"Hola, amor," he heard Mom greet Dad. "How was your day?"

"It ain't stoppin' anytime soon!" Dad answered, taking off his holster. "Kids are floating over in cheap dinghies in broad daylight, then waiting for us to get them. The chief's saying all the processing centers are bursting at the seams. Forecast is ninety thousand unaccompanied minors by year's end. Today we had a hundred and fourteen!"

Frank heard this number and ran to his room to adjust the growing column of illegals caught by the Rio Grande Valley Sector in the graph he had started a year ago. He kept it in his secret notebook hidden under the mattress so Mom wouldn't see it. He figured she wouldn't understand. But Frank wanted to keep a tally of all the bad people Dad apprehended. The kids were coming from Honduras, Guatemala, and El Salvador, and for some weird reason the government couldn't send them back to where they came from right away like they could the Mexicans. These kids had to see a judge or something to approve their staying or leaving. If it were up to Frank he would have flung them right back. Some of the kids, Frank had heard, didn't even know Spanish. What did they speak? Frank was fluent in two languages. Mom and Gramps had taught him Spanish. Gramps called these aliens *indiecitos ignorantes*. He said the ignorant Indians were a real burden on society.

At dinner, Dad was mostly silent as he ate a second helping of Mom's *chili con carne*. Mom did most of the talking, going on and on about the new exhibit she was helping curate at the Mission Historical Museum. She was all about the history of Texas. Frank got up to clear the table when Dad had finished eating.

"Dad," Frank asked, "can we go to the shooting range?"

"No seas insistente," said Mom. "How many times have you asked your father the same

question this week? Dad is tired. And he needs to go back to work tonight. They're short on staff."

Dad had been working overtime since the surge of kids began, and it was taking a toll on him. Frank hated that he didn't get as much time with his Dad as he used to. He hated the illegal kids for it.

"Come here, Frank," said Dad. Frank went over to stand by Dad's side. "Tell ya what, I have a break tomorrow afternoon. We'll go check out the range then. How 'bout that?"

"Thank you, Dad!" Frank hugged his father.

The next day Frank woke up at dawn, wide-eyed with excitement. He had dreamed of guns and targets. He vaguely remembered hearing the front door closing during his sleep. Dad must have returned late. By two o'clock Frank was pacing in his room, his slingshot in the left pocket of his cargo shorts. Finally Dad woke up and, after a bite to eat, made good on his promise. They climbed into the family van in the hundred-degree heat. Frank was itching to get to the gun range.

"Don't have too much fun!" Mom called from the doorway, a hint of worry in her voice.

It was a short ride to the indoor shooting range on West Two Mile Road. Frank and Dad took their places in the registration line behind a big woman and two kids who couldn't have been more than eight.

Dad rented a 9 mm gun and taught Frank how to safely handle, hold, and aim it. Frank nodded after each of Dad's instructions. An hour and a half later, Frank was tired. Managing the gun's recoil was not easy. He had been able to hit the paper silhouette of the man thirty feet away most of the time and was proud of his first effort. So they called it a day.

"You're a good shot, boy!" Dad said. "Look at that cluster of bullet holes!" He high-fived Frank.

Frank grinned all the way back to the van. The temperature had dropped slightly, and the blue of the sky had deepened.

"Dad, can you take me to where you caught the illegal aliens yesterday?" asked Frank.

"Call them immigrants, son, you hear me?" said Dad.

"Okay," sighed Frank. "Can you? Please?"

"All right," Dad replied.

They rode for half an hour to a wildlife refuge by the river. Anzalduas Park was usually full on weekends. It was almost empty on this Thursday afternoon. Dad drove up the road and parked not far from the dam. Frank was no longer tired, and he jumped out of the car and swaggered behind Dad all the way to where the trees met the dam. Dozens of lacy dragonflies flew in front of Frank, but he didn't notice them. He could not stop staring at the river and its invisible borderline. The same rushing water had two names: Río Bravo to the south, Rio Grande to the north.

"Right over there. See the trees on the other side that are like a cove by the river?" Dad asked.

"That's where whole groups gather before crossing over. The border is so close to us we can't do nothing until they're almost here."

Frank instinctively scanned the river for illegals, feeling like one of his superheroes. Suddenly he saw something in the distance.

"There!" he said. He pointed to a couple of heads bobbing in the water. "Can we arrest them?"

Dad squinted his eyes. "Naw, that's just people swimming, not trying to cross. Even if they were, I'm off duty, son."

"Aw." Frank sighed again.

"Let's go back," said Dad. "I need to check on something."

They returned to the van and drove out of the park. On 396, Dad slowed down at the sight of a Border Patrol truck parked in front of Crazy Joe's Saloon. He pulled in next to it.

"Stay here," said Dad. "I'll be back soon."

Frank heard a commotion inside the rickety wooden building and craned his neck out the window. Men's voices could be heard inside. Frank opened the car door and peered over it, shielding his eyes with his left hand from the setting sun. From this vantage point he could see a uniformed agent out back on the saloon's patio talking to women with babies and a bunch of children who didn't look clean. He saw Dad join the large group. Suddenly Frank heard a rustle on the right side of the wooden building. His heart skipped a beat. He wasn't supposed to leave the car. He heard the rustle again. He couldn't resist. He needed to take action. He got out of the car, closed the door without making a noise, and tiptoed his way to the side of the saloon.

Frank sensed movement, and he inched forward. He retrieved his slingshot from one pocket and his ammo from another. He could do this! A few yards away, torn green tennis shoes poked out from the corner of the building. Just like he thought—an illegal alien must be hiding here. He would show Dad *he* could catch one! Frank readied his slingshot. He brought it to a full draw before raising his arms and aiming at his target. Just as he was about to release the ammo, a song, a string of beautiful, unrecognizable words, reached him. Frank lowered his arms, dazzled by the melody. And he walked to its source, curious.

Turning the corner, Frank found a girl. She had her black hair braided and carried a small bag. She gazed up, her almond eyes as golden as her skin. On her lap she held a vibrant drawing. She smiled, and the tiniest wrinkles formed around her nose.

"¿La utz awach?" she said.

Frank did not understand a word.

"Ri in nub'i' Romina," the girl added, pointing to herself. *"Ri in nub'i' Romina."*

Frank thought she was saying her name.

"Soy Frank," Frank said, pointing to himself and smiling back at the intriguing girl. "I'm Frank."

"'S-o-y'? Soy Romina." The girl pointed to

herself. "Frank." She giggled, pointing to Frank.

A quick learner, Frank thought, surprised. As Romina rose from the ground, she dropped her drawing. Frank picked it up and stared at it for a long time. He had never seen so many swirling colors forming such a fantastic landscape. It was a picture of a blue river at the foot of lush green mountains sprinkled with pink and yellow houses. But the blue river wasn't really blue, because it was made with swirling stripes of aqua and green and pink and violet. And the green mountains were drawn with swirling stripes of yellow and aqua and blue and lavender. The only black-and-white thing in the drawing was the skirt of the girl in the foreground. She walked barefoot down the hill and was bent over under the weight of the load of wood she carried on her back. Frank handed the drawing back to Romina, looking at her with a mixture of awe and admiration.

"Muy bonito," Frank said, gesturing to the drawing. "Very pretty." He couldn't help smiling

at this girl. She held his complete attention.

"Bo-ni-to." Romina giggled. "Pre-tty."

Romina opened her bag, searching for something in it.

Just then Frank heard his father calling. And Dad's voice brought Frank back to reality. Frank shook his head, wanting to break the spell he was under. He had forgotten that Romina was most likely illegal.

"Here, Dad! Come here; I found one!"

Dad came over, followed by the agent on duty.

"What's going on?" they both asked.

Romina took a folded card out of her bag. She gave it to the agent in uniform, looking straight at him with a smile. The name and address of her aunt in Providence, Rhode Island, was written on it. As was the name of the Mayan dialect Romina spoke: K'iche'. Dad and his colleague looked at each other. Dad walked away, talking on his cell phone as the agent led Romina to join the group.

After just a few steps, Romina turned around

and called Frank by name. She handed him her beautiful drawing.

Two days later, Frank sat leaning against his bed, inking another superhero. All his black line drawings were full of angles. He felt the need to look at Romina's drawing again. He pulled it out of its hiding place in his secret notebook. Even though it had been drawn with crayons on cheap paper, it was truly striking. He remembered Romina's golden eyes. There was something about her that made him wish to see her again. He stroked Romina's signature on her drawing with the tip of his finger and felt a deep longing. And then he was ashamed. She was beneath him. Or was she? Was it wrong to feel this way? Did it matter that she was not from a good old Spanish family like Gramps said Frank was? Frank sensed that he and Romina would be friends if they were classmates in Mission. He was so immersed in his thoughts that he didn't hear Mom come into his room with a pile of clean laundry.

"*¡Qué bonito dibujo!*" Mom exclaimed. "Did you make it? *¡Déjame ver!* Let me see!"

Startled, Frank hid Romina's drawing and showed Mom his pen-and-ink art instead. But Mom didn't fall for it. She kept probing until Frank told her in short bursts all about Romina. He told Mom how they had met and how mixed-up he felt about this girl.

Mom sat next to Frank at the foot of his bed and placed her hand on his.

"Frank, you think you're above others because of those stories Gramps tells you," Mom said. "*Y está mal.* It's wrong. *Mi padre*, he doesn't even know the truth. And you should learn about it."

"What do you mean?" Frank asked, puzzled.

"*Bueno,*" Mom said. "It's all in a letter your great-great-aunt sent me a while back. She's the family's genealogist. Wait here."

Mom left the room for a moment. When she returned, she had three pages handwritten in a script that must have taken years of calligraphy exercises to achieve. Mom read the letter aloud. There was a line that Frank asked Mom to repeat several times: *Sólo el que carga el costal sabe lo que lleva adentro.* He memorized it. He wanted to transcribe this Mexican saying later: *Only he who carries the sack knows what it holds.* The letter cited historical sources that documented the ancestry of Mom's mother, Gramps's wife, all the way back to the 1820s, to the Republic of Mexico. She was a descendant of the union between one of the Spanish governors of Mexico and a Mayan Indian woman. This fact had remained a guarded secret for generations, Mom explained. All high-society families valued the purity of the blood. And now here was his family history in plain sight for Frank to ponder what all this meant for him. He jumped to his feet and started pacing around the room. His hands turned to fists inside his pockets. Frank despised the bad people crossing the river. He could hear Gramps in his head saying, *The worst are the* indiecitos ignorantes.

"Am I a mix of Spaniard and Mayan?" Frank asked under his breath. How was this possible?

"Frank," Mom said. "You have nothing to be ashamed of."

He looked at Mom, wanting to understand, wanting to be cool with it. But he just couldn't. He needed to shoot some targets.

A few weeks later Frank was back at the shooting range with Dad. He loved hanging out with him. As they waited to register, Frank remembered the talk with Mom. Once he had calmed down that afternoon, he had gone back inside to transcribe the saying onto the back of Romina's drawing. Frank had spent many days trying to understand how these words related to him. Initially the knowledge of having a Mayan ancestor chipped away at the image Frank had of himself. But after reading some of the books on the Mayan civilization Mom borrowed from the library for him, something started shifting inside. He began to see things differently.

"Here you go," Dad said, making Frank focus on the task at hand. "Steady."

"Yes, Dad." Frank raised the gun with both hands and aimed at the target. And he noticed that the rage he used to feel when shooting had lessened. Frank had recently learned that some of the kids crossing the border were escaping violence in their countries.

"Dad?" asked Frank. "Do you treat all people crossing the border the same?"

"It's an important duty to protect the American way of life," Dad said. "You have to follow the code of conduct, though. It's not an easy job, Frank. Specially when you're dealing with kids."

It was the last day of summer and Frank was at Anzalduas Park again, this time with Mom. She sat at a picnic table, reading under the shade of the trees, which dripped with Spanish moss. Dad had to work—on a Sunday—again. Frank took a soda out of the cooler and went over to the fishing dock.

He gazed at the Rio Grande in front of him, but this time he didn't scan it with anger. He had gone a few more times to the shooting range with Dad. He loved spending time with him, and still wanted to one day be a Border Patrol agent. But now he didn't think that all people who crossed the river were bad. He thought again about how hard it must be to travel alone, not speaking the language, afraid of the Mexican gangs that at any moment could hurt you, extort money from you, or even kill you. It dawned on him that Romina was not only talented; she was courageous. He asked himself if he would have had the same courage if he were in her place. Little by little, Frank had come to realize that he was proud of having Mayan blood running through his veins. Gramps was wrong. Now Frank felt richer by being a mix.

He trashed the empty soda can and walked back to Mom's table, wondering about the letter he had written to Romina. During the Border Patrol's summer barbecue, he had given it to the translator who had helped process and release Romina from custody. Frank had written a few sentences at the bottom of a pen and ink drawing he had created especially for her. He had asked her to teach him a little K'iche'. Fearing Dad's disapproval, Frank hadn't mentioned the letter to him. What if Dad thought he was doing something wrong? Frank slid his hands into his pockets. He still carried his slingshot in one of them, but he sometimes forgot the ammo. The park was full of families enjoying themselves before the start of school. Frank noticed the green jays flying about. And, as he got closer to Mom's table, he could see that she had set it for three. Frank arched his eyebrows in puzzlement. And then he saw Dad in the distance. Frank raced to meet him.

"Dad!"

On a flowered tablecloth Mom had spread grilled Tex-Mex chicken wraps, *nopalitos* salad, chorizo-stuffed chilies, and slices of cold watermelon. Frank grabbed a watermelon slice and sat across from Dad and Mom.

"How come you're here, Dad?"

"What? Want me to go?"

"No!" hollered Frank.

"I switched duty with a friend," said Dad. "I didn't want to miss supper with y'all! It's back to school tomorrow for you."

"Yeah," Frank said. "Summer sure flew by."

"Hey, son, remember the Mayan girl from Crazy Joe's?"

"Yeah?" Frank looked at Mom, who looked away.

"I saw the translator today. He's been in touch with social services in Providence. It looks like the girl is doing okay."

"Um," said Frank. He bit into his watermelon, not wanting to meet Dad's eyes.

"Anyway, I have a letter she wrote back," Dad

said as he slid an envelope across the table. "Want it?"

Frank gulped his food. "Oh," he mumbled.

"Sure glad you took an interest in her," said Dad. "These kids have gone through a lot, ya know?"

Frank looked at his Dad and nodded. Then Frank opened the envelope under the table. Inside, he found a drawing. It had a blue river surrounded by many tall gray buildings. But the blue river wasn't really blue, because it was made with swirling stripes of aqua and green and pink and violet. And the buildings weren't really gray, because they were made with squares and rectangles of ivory and tan and blue and lavender. In the foreground a girl with long black hair looked straight at the viewer, a snow cone in her hand. Three greetings were written one above the other in a column next to the girl's face: *¿La utz awach?*, *hola*, and *hello*. It was signed *Romina*.

Frank stared at the drawing for a long time. He caressed the girl's face and smiled. He folded the drawing and gently slipped it into its envelope, and then he slid the envelope into the pocket of his cargo shorts. Looking up, Frank lifted his eyes to Dad and then Mom. They were both smiling at him.

ACKNOWLEDGMENTS

I am indebted to friends and acquaintances who throughout the years have shared bits of their lives with me, shedding light on difficult issues that touch young Latinos. I am thankful to the dedicated journalists whose articles inspired and informed the stories in this book.

I'm most grateful to medical doctors Arturo E. Betancourt and Anastacio De Castro for their careful review of the stories that explore medical conditions.

Muchísimas gracias to my daughter, Verónica

E. Betancourt, for her invaluable insight and help in the development of the collection. You are a great developmental editor.

I'm especially grateful to my editor, Rosemary Brosnan, for her unshakable faith in me and her insistence in asking for more than I ever thought I could give. Without her trust this book would have been quite different. I also thank the talented and skilled editorial and design teams at Harper-Collins for their brilliant ideas, adroit comments, and for making me feel that the production of the book could not have been in better hands.

Thank you, *gracias, merci*, to the photographers whose pictures inspired many of the portraits in the collection. I appreciate the generosity of Heart to Heart Children's Village in Honduras, a non-profit organization that cares for children like those in my stories.

To the members of my critique group: Jennifer O'Connell, Susan Stockdale, and Janet Stoeke, as always, thank you for the "extra eyes."

TRANSLATIONS OF SPANISH WORDS AND PHRASES

The Attack

m'hijo: my son

sí: yes

fútbol: soccer

una estrella del fútbol: a soccer star

¡Qué bueno!: Great!

milagros: miracles

la Virgen de Guadalupe: the Virgin of
    Guadalupe

gracias: thank you

¡Ay, Diosito mío!: Oh my God!

Vamos a rezar: Let's pray

niños: children

mis milagros: my miracles

Selfie

El pueblo de Los Angeles: the town of Los Angeles (a historical site in Los Angeles, CA)

¡Ay, niño!: Oh, child!

abuelo: grandfather

¿Estás loca?: Are you crazy?

hola: hello

mami: mom

¿Qué voy a hacer contigo?: What am I going to do with you?

Día de los Muertos: the Day of the Dead

fiesta: party

calacas: skeletons

calaveras: skulls

¡Felicidades!: Congratulations!

Güera

colita: small ponytail

la familia: the family

chaparro: shorty

cho-co-cho-co-con-ají: chocolate with hot
   pepper (using the first syllables of the word
   for chocolate)
azabache: jet; a black gemstone
tíos: uncles; in the text it refers to uncles and
   aunts
abuelos: grandparents
de cariño: lovingly
güera: Mexican term for "blonde girl"
Cho-co-cho-co-cho-co-güe-ra: chocolate, blonde
   (using the first syllables of the word for
   chocolate)
A que no se da cuenta la güerita: I'm sure the
   little blonde won't notice
Vé, charla: Go, chat
Tú se lo quitas: You take it
cada palabra: each word
cho-co-cho-co-cho-co-DUL-ce: sweet chocolate
   (using the first syllables of the word for
   chocolate)
cho-co-chi-ca-con-a-JÍ: chocolate, girl with chili

pepper (using the first syllables of the word for chocolate)

Burrito Man

m'hijita: my little daughter

Papi: Dad

por favor: please

Sí, sí, m'hijita, ya verás: Yes, yes, my little daughter, you'll see

refritos: refried beans

cortadito: among Cubans, espresso with a shot of milk

buenos días: good morning

tu favorito: your favorite

¡Hasta mañana!: See you tomorrow!

demasiado tarde: too late

Band-Aid

tres leches: three milks; a Latin American dessert made with three kinds of milk

¿Aló?: Hello?

mi amor: my love

mi hermanita: my little sister

linda: pretty

la gran madre: the Great Mother

Ay, Diosito santo: Oh my God

la migra: immigration police

Sí, sí, entiendo: Yes, yes, I understand

resanbinsi: Honduran rice and bean dish made
  with coconut milk

Firstborn

locura: craziness

mofongo: savory green plantain dish popular
  in Puerto Rico

Ay, bendito: Oh, dear

nena: girl

tu hermana: your sister

¿Verdad?: true; in the text: Isn't it so?

seguro: sure

coquí: small tree frog from Puerto Rico named
  after its song

Es postre: It's for dessert

tostones: double-fried green plantain fritters

¡Feliz cumpleaños!: Happy birthday!

*Feliz, feliz en tu día, amiguita que Dios te
    bendiga*: Birthday song in Puerto Rico; "Be
    happy, happy today, little friend, may God
    bless you . . ."

Luci tiene razón: Luci is right

Cubano Two

Cubanos: Cubans

Tum, pakatum, pakatum, pantum:
    onomatopoeic words

cumbia: cumbia; called the musical backbone
    of Latin America, it predates salsa and
    other Latin rhythms

Sudamérica: South America

Norteamérica: North America

¡Rica azúcaaa'!: Delicious sugar!

resolver: fix (in Cuban dialect, to patch things
    up until the next crisis)

chiquitico: little one (in Cuban dialect)

iguales: the same

oye.: listen

música: music

vacilón: someone who enjoys having a good
time (colloquial word)

sázon: seasoning

Peacemaker

Abu: *abu* is short for *abuela*

Purísima: Immaculate (in Nicaragua, this
refers to the beloved Virgin Mary and her
feast day)

gofio: Nicaraguan candy

Titi: Auntie

Tío: Uncle

buñuelos: sweet deep-fried fritters popular in
Latin America

pan dulce: sweet bread

un hombrecito: a young man

todo un hombrecito: a real young man

cafecito: little coffee; often it refers to an
expresso or shot of strong coffee

The Secret

Te tengo que contar algo: I need to tell you
something

Nada de trabajo, nada: No work at all, none

coyote: jackal; term used to describe the
person who enables illegal border crossing
for a fee

nada: nothing

¡Mentirosa!: Liar!

Dulcería Lupitas: Lupita's Sweets Shop (a
Latin American sweets store in Chicago)

paleta de tamarindo: tamarind lollipop

salón de belleza: beauty parlor

Selecciones: Spanish version of *Reader's Digest*

¿Qué pasa?: What's going on?

abuelo: grandfather

paletas: lollipops

¡Tamarindo!: Tamarind!

Pickup Soccer

¡Órale!: Let's go! (Mexican exclamation)

Saturday School

Escuela Argentina: Argentinean school

¿Te pasa algo?: What's going on with you?

¡Vas a aprender mucho aquí!: You'll learn a lot
here!

¿Tú sabes dónde me siento?: Do you know
where should I sit?

¿Y vos, cómo te llamás?: And you, what's your
name?

Me llamo Sandra: My name is Sandra

Buenos días, chicos: Good morning, children

Buenos días, Señora Peña: Good morning,
Mrs. Peña

*Ché, Mauricio, encontrále un pupitre a la chica
nueva, ¿querés?*: Hey, Mauricio, find the new
girl a desk, will you?

¿Sos Sandra, no?: You're Sandra, right?

¡Mirá sus orejas!: Look at her ears.

Sandra, vení, a almorzar: Sandra, come on over to lunch

Cúentame: Tell me

Vos, no sabés lo que aprendí yo: You have no idea what I learned

90,000 Children

mojados: wet (illegal immigrants who have crossed US–Mexico border on foot)

un verdadero: a real one

indiecitos ignorantes: ignorant Indians

chili con carne: chili

No seas insistente.: Don't be pushy.

¿La utz awach?: Hello? (in K'iche')

Ri in nub'i' Romina.: My name is Romina. (in K'iche')

Soy Frank.: I'm Frank.

muy bonito: very pretty

K'iche': Mesoamerican language in the Mayan family

¡Qué bonito dibujo!: What a beautiful drawing!

¡Déjame ver!: Let me see!

Y está mal: And it's wrong

mi padre: my father

bueno: well

nopalitos: prickly pear; cactus used as a
   vegetable in recipes

TRANSLATIONS OF
THE <u>REFRANES</u>

Refranes are sayings in the Spanish language that often convey a lot in a succinct way.

The Attack

De noche todos los gatos son pardos.

At night, all cats are black.

Selfie

El que quiera celeste, que le cueste.

He who aims for heaven must work for it.

Güera

Las apariencias engañan.

Appearances deceive.

Burrito Man

Nadie sabe el bien que tiene hasta que lo pierde.

No one knows his wealth until he loses it.

Band-Aid

No se puede tapar el cielo con la mano.

You can't hide the sky with one hand.

Firstborn

Hay que coger al toro por los cuernos.

One must take the bull by the horns.

Cubano Two

Tal para cual.

The one for the other.

Peacemaker

Las aguas siempre vuelven a su cauce.

River waters always return to their bed.

The Secret

Mañana será otro día.

Tomorrow will be another day.

Pickup Soccer

El fútbol es la única religión que no tiene ateos.

Soccer is the only religion without atheists.

Saturday School

*Ser valiente es tener miedo a quedarse sin
hacer nada.*

Being brave is to be afraid of doing nothing.

90,000 Children

*Sólo el que carga el costal sabe lo que lleva
adentro.*

Only he who carries the sack knows what it
holds.

NOTES ON THE STORIES

I set almost every story squarely where it happened after researching the locale described in the news item that inspired it. However, for the stories based on events that happened to friends or acquaintances, I chose to set them in places different from where they occurred, out of respect for people's privacy. I consulted both the Census Bureau and the Migration Policy Institute in order to find a state and city with a large amount of the particular Latino population I was writing about. All the real names of people have been changed. The articles that inspired or informed each story have been cited under its title.

The Attack

This story retells Guadalupe's account of events that occurred in 2007. Although Guadalupe's family members were either legal residents or citizens of the United States, all contributing members to society, they felt profiled and unwelcome. And even though her story was never reported, many others who recount similar instances of police abuse have appeared in the national news since then.

Kelly, Kimbriell, Sarah Childress, and Steven Rich. "Forced Reforms, Mixed Results." *Washington Post.* November 15, 2015. Print.

Selfie

For years I had been hearing about the problem of obesity among the poor, the difficulty of good nutrition on a budget, and the incidence of type 2 diabetes among Latinos. The insulin resistance condition is prevalent in the overweight and may cause constant thirst, tiredness, and blurry vision.

Prediabetes has almost no warning signs except sometimes for the condition *Acanthosis nigricans.* Common among people of African, Caribbean, Pacific Islander, and Hispanic descent, the condition presents as patches of thick velvety dark skin around creases and folds. It often looks like dirt that can't be washed off. If I explored these issues in a story, would the main character be able to find a solution even within her life's difficult circumstances? I found the way out for Marla when I heard about the Eastside Bike Club on National Public Radio.

Archer, Edward. "We Can't Blame Obesity on Our Genes." *Washington Post.* June 16, 2015. Print.

Medina, Jennifer. "Los Angeles Neighborhood Tries to Change, but Avoid the Pitfalls." *New York Times.* August 17, 2013. http://www.nytimes.com/2013/08/18/us/los-angeles-neighborhood-tries-to-change-but-avoid-the-pitfalls.html?_r=0

Meraji, Shereen Marisol. "On A 'Tour De Tacos' With

Los Angeles' Eastside Bike Club." *National Public Radio*. July 26, 2015. http://www.npr.org/sections/codeswitch/2015/07/26/425659877/on-a-tour-de-tacos-with-los-angeles-eastside-bike-club.

Saslow, Eli. "All Eyes on the 8th: D.C. Family Adjusts after Cuts to Monthly Food Stamps It Relies On." *Washington Post*. December 16, 2013. Print.

Saslow, Eli. "Too Much of Too Little: A Diet Fueled by Food Stamps is Making South Texans Obese but Leaving them Hungry." *Washington Post*. November 10, 2013. Print.

Güera

There is wide misconception among the people of the United States that all Latinos are brown and most are poor. I wanted to dispel this notion by portraying the phenomenon of mistaken identity some Latinos living in the US experience. I intended to show that we hail from varied socio-economic backgrounds and come in many shades. In this story, Güera ends up owning the nickname she initially disliked, and comes to be proud of who she is.

Booth, William, and Nick Miroff. "Mexico's Middle-Class Migrants." *Washington Post*. July 24, 2012. Print.

Burrito Man

As soon as I read Steve Hendrix's story I knew it would inspire a story for children. It touches on themes relevant to many: persistence, grief, hard work as the key to success, and the discovery that an otherwise unassuming person was such a contributing member to society. What I didn't know was that in writing this story, the second one after "The Attack," I would continue on to write ten more.

Hendrix, Steve. "A Hole in Their Hearts, and Stomachs: Farragut Square Mourns a Man who Began as a Vendor, Became a Friend." *Washington Post*. October 7, 2010. Print.

Band-Aid

The issue of mixed-status America is a difficult one. Exploring what it means for a young girl to have her life change drastically because of a parent's deportation was sobering to me. Eli Saslow's article sheds light on an extraordinary woman, and I chose to have *la gran madre*'s story as the background for Elena's trials.

Saslow, Eli. "A '*Band-Aid*' for 800 Children." *Washington Post*. July 6, 2014. Print.

Firstborn

One is not always aware of having a bully in the family. It is a difficult thing to accept and deal with. For a newly arrived Spanish speaker it's even harder, since no equivalent of the word *bully* exists in the Spanish language. The events that happened to Luci truly happened to a very close friend of mine. This friend, unlike Luci, didn't realize her sibling was a bully until late into her adult life.

Bullyonline.org. "Bullying in the Family." May 4, 2015.
  http://bullyonline.org/index.php/13-bullying-at-
  home/130-bullying-in-the-family.
Jordan, Mary. "Exodus from Puerto Rico Could Sway
  Election." *Washington Post*. July 27, 2015. Print.
Kennedy, Kerry. "An End to Bullying." *Washington Post*.
  August 12, 2013. Print.

Cubano Two

For years I've heard the different viewpoints from family and friends who hail from Cuba about the reasons behind the waves of migration. My own father-in-law was Cuban. Rather than delve deeply into the complexities of these issues, I chose to offer a glimpse in a story that would make readers laugh, and perhaps prompt them to find out more about Cuban migration.

Miroff, Nick. "Change Coming to Cuba in Fits and Starts."
  Washington Post. December 16, 2015. Print.
Rennie, David. "Cuba Libre." *The Economist Special
  Report: America's Hispanics*. March 14, 2015. Print.

Peacemaker

Both the character of Wilfred and the difficult issues he needs to deal with are based on the life of a very close friend of mine. And although this story is open-ended, in real life my friend remained the peacemaker until his parents' passing. Dysfunctional families abound, and neither your ethnicity nor your social status shields you.

Neu, Denese. "The Story of La Purísima and La Griteria: A Unique Nicaraguan Sacred Tradition Adapted to Louisiana." Louisiana Folklife Program. http://www.louisianafolklife.org/LT/Articles_Essays/nicaraguans.html

Ware, Carolyn. "Ritual Spaces in Traditional Louisiana Communities: Italian, Nicaraguan, and Vietnamese Altars." Louisiana Folklife Program. http://www.louisianafolklife.org/LT/Articles_Essays/creole_art_ritual_spaces.html.

The Secret

I closely followed the news about the Dream Act as the administration was discussing it in 2011 and 2012. Reading Julia Preston's article made me want to consider the feelings and events that one young girl experienced, which led her to stand along with thousands of other young Latinos in Chicago.

Foley, Elise. "Deferred Action Immigration Event Draws Thousands of Dreamers on First Day." August 15, 2012. http://www.huffingtonpost.com/2012/08/15/deferred-action-immigration_n_1785443.html

Hendrix, Steve and Luz Lazo. "Reform Changes Little for Many." *Washington Post.* August 16, 2012. Print.

Markon, Jerry. "Migrant Flow at Border Abates." *Washington Post.* May 28, 2015. Print.

Preston, Julia. "Illegal Immigrants Line Up by Thousands for Deportation Deferrals." *New York Times.* August 15, 2012. http://www.nytimes.com/2012/08/16/us/illegal-immigrants-line-up-for-deportation-deferrals.html.

Pickup Soccer

All across the United States, city neighborhoods are going through gentrification. It's an issue that may bring positives as well as negatives. Gentrification often displaces longtime residents. When I heard about this San Francisco incident on National Public Radio, I thought it was the perfect story to highlight the subject and its consequences. I examined what it means for a young boy to find himself with ties to both the neighborhood kids and the gentrifiers, and I relished telling the story in a manner that incorporates the energy and excitement of soccer within the written form.

Meraji, Shereen Marisol. "ICYMI 2014: Soccer Field Standoff Highlights Gentrification Tension." *National Public Radio*. December 27, 2014. http://www.npr.org/sections/codeswitch/2014/12/27/373284989/icymi-2014-soccer-field-standoff-highlights-gentrification-tension.

Wong, Julia Carrie. "Dropbox, Airbnb, and the Fight Over San Francisco's Public Spaces." *New Yorker*. October

23, 2014. http://www.newyorker.com/tech/elements/
dropbox-airbnb-fight-san-franciscos-public-spaces.

Saturday School

Many youngsters born in the United States to parents who are proud of their heritage and language
of birth are encouraged to study it on Saturdays.
It is through language that one gains full access
to a culture. I decided to explore this notion in
the context of a family with several generations,
each speaking a different kind of Spanish. Born to
Argentinean parents in Puerto Rico, I often felt I
lived in two countries: the one within the confines
of my home, and the one beyond them. This story
is based on true events.

Rennie, David. "Dreaming in English." *The Economist
Special Report: America's Hispanics*. March 14, 2015.
Print.

90,000 Children

The surge of unaccompanied minors crossing the border in 2014 elicited a barrage of articles tackling the subject. I read many of them and chose to examine the issue from the viewpoint of a middle-class and quite prejudiced Tejano boy. This choice allowed me to explore deeply ingrained misconceptions among some Latinos.

Farrah, Douglas. "5 Myths About the Border Crisis." *Washington Post*. August 10, 2014. Print.

Markon, Jerry and Joshua Partlow. "Unaccompanied Children Surging Anew Across Southwest U.S. Border." *Washington Post*. December 17, 2015. Print.

Nakamura, David. "Migrant Influx Frustrates Border Agents." *Washington Post*. June 22, 2014. Print.

"Under-age and on the Move." *The Economist*. June 28, 2014. Print.